Stories

Introduction 7
Anne Caldwell

My Mother Dreams of Lovelace Watkins 9
Nell Farrell

Talking to My Mother on the Intercom 33
River Wolton

Visit to the Psychotherapist 55
Anne Caldwell

The Importance of Tea – and Rabbits 75
Char March

The Gorge 95
Suzanne Batty

Mother 107
Clare Shaw

Some Girls' Mothers

Suzanne Batty
Anne Caldwell
Nell Farrell
Char March
Clare Shaw
River Wolton

route

First published by Route
PO Box 167, Pontefract, WF8 4WW
info@route-online.com
www.route-online.com

ISBN (13): 978-1-901927-39-9
ISBN (10): 1-901927-39-3

Editor:
Anne Caldwell

Thanks to:
Ian Daley and Isabel Galan at Route, Polly Thomas, Ann Atkinson, Gillie Bolton, Helen Drucquer, Clare Maguire, Fiona Outram, Betsy Warland, Barbara Skillen, Simon Midgeley, Jane Mathieson, Rose Ryan, Libby Tempest, Janet Puzylo, Anne Sherman, Punam Ramchurn, Catherine Browne and Avril Heffernan.

This book is based on real lives and events but is a work of creative non-fiction. Some names and details have been changed. The views expressed are those of the authors themselves.

Cover Design, Art Direction and Photography
made in The Designers Republic
www.thedesignersrepublic.com

A cata ... y

No

Printec ... D

To my mum, Pat, for saying,
when I showed her this piece:
I'm not sure if I'm good or bad,
but I loved it anyway

To Jenny Wolton, with love and thanks for
lessons in rule-breaking and style

Alice Caldwell

To Ma (Joyce Motley) for all
our brilliant times together,
and for everything she's taught me

To Niamh and to my
mother with gratitude

Introduction

This collection of six stories is a celebration of love. The pieces of writing are like windows on a rambling house, populated by many different mothers and daughters: some you may recognise, some you may find illuminating and new to you. There are acts of rebellion and acts of tenderness. The daughters in this book are bold, sensitive, questioning and often concerned with finding common ground with their mothers or finding a new way of communicating.

What does it mean to be a daughter? How do the relationships with our mothers develop? These are two very complex questions. Louise Guinness, editor of *The Vintage Book of Fathers*, writes that 'each generation finds fault with the methods their parents used to bring them up, each generation determines not to make the same mistakes.' This is true of my own relationship with my mother, but getting older and becoming a mother myself has led to me to discover the values that I share with her.

What links the authors of this book is that we are primarily poets, exploring our lives in prose together for the first time. This is reflected in the luminous language and its sensory richness. Many of the stories explore the body, either our own, our daughters' or our mothers' physical selves.

As we grow up, do we turn into our mothers or turn away from them? This book shows that there is no straightforward answer and that the truth is complex. There were tears and laughter as we wrote together and shared our work. We hope you enjoy the results.

Anne Caldwell

My Mother Dreams of Lovelace Watkins

Nell Farrell

You are standing in the kitchen peeling potatoes. If you were making chips I'd know exactly what would happen next. It is one of the few things we do in the same way.

Your hands are different to mine, larger, plumper, every fingernail bitten to its sore, embedded quick. I have tiny hands, am smaller than you altogether, have inherited your own mother's restless, bustling energy around the house. But in the making of chips, we are as one. We peel thickly, rather than paring and then we slice the potato into rounds. We cut each round along its vertical plane into robust chips, half an inch thick and two to three inches long, depending on the potatoes. Then we soak them in a bowl of cold water.

When the fat in the chip pan is almost smoking, we empty our thick-cut, robust chips onto a clean tea towel and pat them dry. Then we fry them, in an old-fashioned chip pan, with a basket, until they are golden brown and crisp on the outside, fluffy on the inside.

The chips I learned to make by watching you are possibly the most perfect things I ever create. There is nothing else in my life of which I feel so confident and proud; nothing which so unequivocally delights others.

But on this particular occasion you aren't making chips and I am not learning anything about perfection.

I have just walked in the front door from school and I can see you, along the passageway, in front of the sink. The wallpaper is patterned with avocado green and mustard yellow geometric shapes. I have cut up and sellotaped a leftover roll of it around my school textbooks to protect them.

You have your back to me.

'What's Dad having for his tea?'

It's almost always the first thing I ask on getting home from school. There is a list of comfortable responses:

Steak and chips
Pork ribs
Lentil soup
Sausage and onion
Ham hock and mushy peas
Smoked haddock in milk with a poached egg

Today's response is: 'A nice tin of sliced roast beef in gravy with mashed potatoes.'

You continue with your task, finish peeling the potatoes, put two pans of water on to boil. Into one you put the potatoes, with plenty of salt. When the other pan comes to the boil, you lower a large oval tin into it, so that the pre-cooked slices of roast beef immersed in gravy inside can heat through. It is, I suppose, an early 1970s convenience food. There is a picture on the tin of its moist brown contents. You are quiet, focused on your task. A spectator could easily imagine you are preparing your beloved spouse's favourite meal.

I am in the kitchen watching you. I leave the room and then come back. I go upstairs, try to start my homework, come back down again, pace around. Because there is something we both know. My dad hates sliced roast beef in gravy.

Every time you have cooked it for him it has ended up in the bin. A couple of times he has thrown it at the wall. Sometimes, as he has raged in the background, you have tried to persuade him that he loves sliced roast beef in gravy. You've reminded him of the times (entirely invented, or lost in the mists of your unimaginable courtship) when he has eaten and enjoyed it. On other occasions you have been cavalier, telling him you have had no time or (even more incendiary) that he does not give you enough housekeeping to always buy him just what he likes to eat.

You take the tin out of the boiling water and, wrapping one corner in a tea-towel, you open it with the tin-opener. You put some mashed potato on the plate. You spoon out the meat and gravy. You put the plate down in front of my dad.

In the aftermath you act as if something unreasonable and upsetting has occurred. Which, of course it has. But you believe that it has only happened to you.

*

The economics of our household are baroque and patriarchal, modelled on the Vatican perhaps. Money is very short anyway, but there is my dad's money and there is money for the rest of us. Every Friday morning before leaving for work he writes my mum a cheque for her 'housekeeping'. When I'm not at school I go with her into Eastwood. We go to the National Westminster Bank – a palace of shiny wooden counters, queues and boredom – and cash the cheque.

Then, with money in her purse, we wander along Eastwood's main shopping street, calling at the butchers, the bakers, the Co-op and Fine Fare as my mum buys all the food – my dad's individually prepared 'Head of the Household' suppers and the Birds Eye beefburgers, fish fingers and Findus crispy pancakes the other three of us eat. The money often runs out before the end of the week and she borrows from our piggy banks or from my nan.

One year my brother wins some money with a premium bond and he uses it to buy us both shoes. Meanwhile, there is a payment going monthly to Sanders Menswear shop in Eastwood because my dad's job means he has to wear suits. And there are pound notes going into his pocket to spend at the Football Club bar which is the one place where I think he is happy. One of the ways my grandparents help us out – in a situation of which they clearly and openly disapprove – is by buying me and my brother clothes. The winter I am fourteen some kind of re-drawing of the lines happens and the purse is clamped shut. It becomes clear that my dad is going to have to buy our coats that winter – and even clearer that the only way I will get a coat is to find one in Sanders Menswear. Thank God for duffel coats.

One Friday, before a bank holiday – one of those times when everything closes down and people have to buy in all their food for the next few days – we have been to Fine Fare and there is a tin of sliced roast beef in gravy at the bottom of my mum's shopping bag. We have more or less finished. We don't seem to be going to the butcher's. I can feel my heart rate increase, my breathing become shallow. My anxiety fills me up, pushes the words out: 'Are we not going to get some pork or steak or something for Dad's tea? You know he doesn't like…'

She ignores me, keeps walking.

★

My mum is the driver in our family. Anywhere we go in a car my mum is at the wheel, driving my grandpa's Ford Zodiac – or later his Ford Zephyr – beautiful blue cars with dazzlingly lovely names, borrowed for the occasion. Eventually we get our own car – another of the times my grandparents don't put their hands in their pockets to bail us out. My mum gets a part-time job in an insurance office, above a barber's shop with a proper red and white stripy pole. She types and does shorthand. I get her to show me her notebook – squiggles and lines and circles; magic writing that I can make no sense of. It is always something boring like *Dear Sir, with regard to your letter of the 14th*, made beautiful and mysterious by this code she knows. From what she earns, she saves up and buys a second-hand black Morris Minor.

Sometimes on our trips into Eastwood, after the bank and the shops, the car takes a sharp right-hand turn and heads down Victoria Street, the steep terraced row where DH Lawrence was born. But we aren't making a literary pilgrimage.

We pull into a courtyard and park the car, walk through double doors into a darkened dusty barroom which smells of beer and cigarette ash. A working men's social club with a betting shop in the courtyard. *My daddy's club* my mum says, in her working-class princess way.

My grandpa, Walter Timmins, part-owner of the Victoria Club, is a short fat man; bespectacled with brilliantined hair and a smart three-piece suit, elasticated bangles holding up his shirt sleeves like a bookie in a thirties gangster movie. His father, Eli Timmins, was a miner, but Walter has made a bit of money from various businesses and been helped along the way by a win on the football pools.

This is where my dad works. My clever, handsome dad, who sings Latin hymns in the bath and teaches me verses from 'The Lady of Shalott'. Who doesn't like me reading comics or saying *Yeah.* Who gets angry if we run out of salt or HP Sauce. Who drinks too much. Who has a degree in English and History from Glasgow University and has been a teacher in Scotland. But who doesn't have a teaching certificate so can't teach in England. Who is so clever he went to university when he was sixteen but had to have a job as well to help his family support him.

My dad is putting his qualifications and his lightning-quick maths to good use calculating odds and taking bets, in grudging and rebellious servitude to his father-in-law. Sometimes he helps out behind the bar; helps Marion, the landlady, wife of Joe; raven-haired like Snow White in the Disney film, making my mum hiss like the Wicked Queen and rattle her bag of poisoned apples. *Your father's fancy woman.* I have absolutely no idea if it's true, but the jealousy and tension are palpable.

When we leave – out of the gloomy room, back through the double doors, out into the courtyard – it's like coming out of the cinema after watching a sad film. That same feeling of surprise that it's still daylight; that same, slight melancholy you can't shake off.

*

The longest drive my mum and I ever took together was to a convent in Leek, Staffordshire. We were going to visit Sister Jacinta. My mum loved Sister Jacinta. She was not alone in this. We all loved her. Every single child at the Priory Roman Catholic primary school, Hilltop, Eastwood; every mother who ever dropped her children off or helped out in the kitchen or on playground duty; every father who was ever dragged to parents' evening.

She was that irresistible combination of fun and no-nonsense. She hitched up the skirt of her habit and kicked a ball around the playground. She raced us on Sports Day. She took my brother on at marbles one playtime and showed no mercy, relieving him of every single one – 'skint' him – and wouldn't give them back even when he cried.

She was fresh-faced, sweet and sharp in equal measure. She could teach just about anyone to read. She was the first person I ever saw fill a kettle by its spout – everyone I knew took the lid off. It had never occurred to me that there was another way of doing it. There was something slightly transgressive about it, especially coming from a nun.

When she was moved to the Leek convent there was universal heartbreak. A petition was sent to the Bishop, but to no avail. Her gifts were needed elsewhere. My mum was determined that we would go and visit her. I think Sister Jacinta knew a lot about how unhappy my mum was sometimes. She was one of those people who always got it right; who listened, said the right things, left people wanting more of her.

I don't remember anything about our visit. I don't remember if it was a nice convent, if the other nuns were friendly, if they gave us cake. I don't remember if my mum and I chatted in the car. We both liked to chat but I'm not sure it's a thing we did much of together. All I remember is that the journey seemed to take forever. It felt like travelling to a different country.

★

It is 1973, a Monday evening. I have the house to myself. The peace is miraculous. I am playing records in the front room. We've been here ten years now and the lounge has just been redecorated. I love being in it, just gazing around at how new and shiny everything is – the carpet with its blocky pattern of green and red and gold and orange; the chandelier we bought in Woolworths; the Baxi Bermuda gas fire, all silvery stainless steel; the brown mock leather sofa with wooden arms and, most of all, the new stereo. The old blue Dansette record player now lives up in my bedroom but tonight I am cruising my mum's records, playing them on the glassy new contraption whose speakers occupy opposite ends of the unit like twins. I do like some of her music – the Beatles, the Walker Brothers.

My mother dreams of Lovelace Watkins. His frilly-shirted, big-voiced, tight-trousered presence is taking over the house. If I don't take care when walking through the front room I will trip over the glossy, purple-covered double album, *Lovelace Watkins Live at the Talk of the Town,* lying open on the floor with all the photos facing outwards. My mum plays it non-stop. She is going to see him at the Commodore Ballroom. She talks about him constantly; gets giddy when he's on the television. A person could very easily become confused about who the teenage girl is in this house.

I am not a fan of Lovelace Watkins – his booming voice, his overblown songs. I am beginning to sense there is a soundtrack to ending up stuck in Eastwood. His music and a lot of the other music my mum likes features on it – Tom Jones, Elvis, the Supremes, the Jackson Five, Stevie Wonder, Ike and Tina Turner.

But something is about to happen.

I pick up one of my mum's singles. Atlantic label, 1973. Fantastic colours – dark turquoise and orange. *Killing Me Softly with His Song* by Roberta Flack. Today, for the first time, I turn it over and listen to the B side.

The needle drops, the introduction begins – strings, piano, a slow, sad, lush beat.

And then – a song unlike anything I have ever heard before, a beautiful bruise of a song:

Nobody feels any pain, tonight as I stand inside of the rain.
Everybody knows, Baby's got new clothes.
Lately I've shown my ribbons and my bows
And my problems...
And I take just like a woman
And I make love, just like a woman
And I ache, just like a woman
I break up like a little girl.

I can't quite work out what's happening, but it hooks me like a good story should. There is something so mysterious and adult and sexy going on:

The Queen Mary is my friend
I believe I'll go and see her again
Ain't nobody has to guess,
That baby won't be blessed
Till she finds out she's just like all the rest
With her problems, her amphetamines and her pearls…

There is something I want very badly in this song – a worldliness that smells of somewhere else. I play it over and over. At some point, maybe in lifting the needle to set it down again or maybe even in lifting the record off to check exactly what it's called, I notice the songwriting credit, a tiny bracketed word off to the left underneath the song title – Dylan.

A few days later I gather up my accumulated babysitting money and head for Woolworths in Eastwood, palace of all things wonderful and exotic to find out more. I buy *Bob Dylan's Greatest Hits.*

★

When I started at my Catholic Girls' Grammar school in Nottingham, two bus-rides away from Eastwood, one of the first things I learnt was that I talked funny.

'Miss Arnold – just listen to how she says *singing*!'

I quickly learned to moderate my accent; not hugely, just enough to not get laughed at. Since then I have brushed up against Hull, Liverpool and now Sheffield accents, the cross-pollination leaving me with a kind of generic 'northern' accent. But my mum has a proper Eastwood accent. It's almost impossible to imitate. Most people don't even realise there is one – just listen to all the cod Yorkshire that clatters through any DH Lawrence dramatisation. An Eastwood accent is an unmistakeable sound. It is actually a recognised and ancient dialect – East Midlands English – with its mouth-filling, chewy vowels and its poetic and essential vocabulary, stretching all the way back to when we were part of the ancient kingdom of Mercia. My mum, a big fan of anxiety and drama, has often just had *a right tatar* and is frequently *wittled to death.* The back garden is often *snided out* with ants in the summer, just as Skegness is *snided out* with people. Children say *scraightin'* instead of crying and we have a brilliant phrase for gathering up our last few pennies to pay for something or pulling a meal together out of nothing – *scrattin' up.* We pride ourselves on not being *nesh* or *mardy*, though stubborn little girls are often *manny.*

★

Recently my mum said to me: 'Well, you were more or less never in the house after about the age of fourteen.'

I was classically dumbfounded – my jaw dropped, my mouth gaped. Exchanges like this aren't uncommon. My mum has a knack of sounding as if she's been given a different script to everyone else in the play. Eventually I managed to ask her where I was then, since as far as I could recall I was either in my bedroom doing my homework like the good Catholic grammar school girl I was, or refereeing her and my dad.

She shrugged and said vaguely, 'Well, you just weren't there...I never felt like I saw you...'

Maybe she is more of a poet than I give her credit for. I think she is remembering and attempting to evoke a feeling of distance between us – which is something I couldn't argue with. I can see it taking shape, wandering around the empty house that night – despising Lovelace Watkins, falling in love with what I saw as a very different kind of song.

Soul music. Amongst all the many other things it is, it is working-class music *par excellence*. The things that matter when you aren't rich or powerful – work, money, dancing, love, sex, food and clothes – all parcelled up with brass and beat and sass; rhyme and rhythm and heartbreak. All that vital uplift and anguish. I wanted none of it. For me as a teenage girl in the 1970s there was a definite split – soul music was sentimental and 'low-brow'. Dylan was cerebral. It was that crude for me – it was secondary modern versus grammar school. It was factory versus university.

Bob Dylan, schooled in the blues, lover of black music, wouldn't recognise the dichotomy. Nor would Roberta Flack, raised on Mahalia Jackson and Sam Cooke but a classically trained pianist, observing no boundaries in her work between jazz, soul and folk. Short on resources though and with a definite sense of how difficult it was all likely to be, hitching my star to the cerebral bandwagon seemed like a way to roll out of Eastwood. Some of the wheels rattled loose along the way, including, mercifully, those fitted by a progressive rock fan boyfriend. But Dylan and me stayed firmly, irrevocably and joyously attached.

★

One of the most important journeys I ever made was unaccompanied. When I was seventeen I packed a couple of bags and trudged up the hill to my grandparents' house. In the bags were clothes of course, but also and most importantly, all the books I needed to study for my 'A' levels. *Wuthering Heights*, *Les Femmes Savantes*, *Der Gute Mensch von Sezuan*; Kafka's stories, Gerard Manley Hopkins' poems, Marguerite Duras's *Moderato Cantabile*; all of us taking up residence at 320 Nottingham Road with my nan and grandpa for the duration of my revision and exams.

This was my master-plan for getting the grades I needed to go to university. Our house was not to be trusted at exam times, as I had learned definitively the night before one of my German 'O' level papers, when the arguing went on deep into the night. I was making sure I had peace and quiet and nowhere was as peaceful for me as my nan's house.

Books in foreign languages might be making their first appearance as I unpacked my bags in the upstairs front bedroom, but it was from my nan's bookcase that I had first taken down *Little Women*, *Jane Eyre*, *Hans Christian Anderson's Fairy Tales* and *A Tale of Two Cities.* The flyleaf of the Dickens was lovingly inscribed *I know of two bright eyes* by a man she didn't marry. If my grandpa was materially aspirational, it was my glamorous ex-barmaid grandma, along with my dad – ironically enough, given their embittered relationship – who showed me that working-class families could love books. As well as stories, she and I would leaf through her two-volume *World's Greatest Paintings*, with its glossy full-colour reproductions. Holman Hunt's *The Light of the World* and Millais's *Boyhood of Raleigh* were her favourites.

When I told her my plan there was no question, no hesitation. When I told my mum and dad no obstacles were put in my way. No one pretended there wasn't a problem; no one pretended we weren't a mess.

I moved in. I revised peacefully every evening after school. At ten o'clock every night my grandpa made us both a mug of Ovaltine and I took mine upstairs where I sat safe and quiet in the spare room double bed, reading thrillers by Ngaio Marsh and Stan Barstow's *A Kind of Loving* trilogy until I fell asleep.

I did my 'A' levels. I got 3 A's. I got away.

★

When I left I took two boxes with me. One was a cardboard box full of the food and basic crockery the University information booklet insisted were vital paraphernalia for living in 'a student house'. The other was a turquoise, plastic-coated box with a carrying handle, a hinged lid and a lock. It contained my record collection. Inside it by then, alongside *Bob Dylan's Greatest Hits*, were other records of his: *Planet Waves*, *Blood on the Tracks* and *Desire.* Keeping them company were records by musicians I had learned were massive Dylan fans – *Greetings from Asbury Park New Jersey*, *The Wild, The Innocent and the E Street Shuffle* and *Born to Run* by Bruce Springsteen, *Horses* by Patti Smith.

Can't Buy a Thrill by Steely Dan was in there, borrowed from a really cool girl at school on the strength of my growing confidence in my own musical taste and *A Salty Dog* by Procol Harum now that I had discovered the delights of second-hand record shops in Nottingham. There was also a collection of the progressive and heavy rock records I listened to with my boyfriend – Yes, Camel,

Atomic Rooster, King Crimson, Wishbone Ash, Focus, Lindisfarne, Genesis.

Nothing that had any discernible relationship with my mum's record collection in the downstairs front room of the house I had just left.

These records somehow gave me an entrée into the bafflingly middle-class world I found myself in. They were looked at, exclaimed over, played and shared around. They gained me enough kudos to survive. What wasn't shared around was the food in my other box. It took me two days to realise that what was considered 'food' in Eastwood literally had no place in this new household.

Around me, young women of my own age or a year or two older, unpacked granary loaves, and bags of Granola. They fried up onions and garlic and green peppers, made wholemeal pizza dough, and quiches. They used pepper that didn't look like fine white dust. They ate yogurt because they liked it, not because they were on a diet. I watched, astonished, entranced and learned very quickly. My box, containing the three tins of baked beans, three tins of Heinz spaghetti and three tins of Plumrose hot dog sausages that my mum and I had bought together in Fine Fare 'to last you till you've settled in and know where the shops are' stayed in my locker in the kitchen. I took them home, undisturbed, at the end of my first term.

My collection of Dylan records grew. Each place I lived had a particular album associated with it. That first year in the student house it was *Highway 61 Revisited*, my vinyl copy of which still bears the stamp *John Sheridan Secondhand Books & Records, Anlaby Road, Hull.* In the house on Hutt Street, where I moved to in my second year with some of the (by now much less scary) girls from my student house, I would listen to *Street Legal* over and over in my tiny room overlooking the street.

I fell in love and moved in with a boy whose very posh mother had always refused to let him eat chips. He introduced me to David Bowie, Joni Mitchell, Neil Young and Leonard Cohen. Our flat echoed to the sounds of Dylan's *Blonde on Blonde* which we both adored. When he came with me on my year in France, we had no record player in our tiny studio apartment, but the poster from Dylan's *Live at Budokan* album adorns the wall in every photo we took.

*

Many years after leaving Eastwood, at some point in the early 1990s, I shared an office with a dancer who needed to have music playing while she worked. I was on my way to the kitchen to make us a cup of tea, when the sheer gorgeousness of a voice and a song stopped me halfway across the floor. My heart was pounding. It was if he'd sung that opening line directly to me. I swivelled on my heels: 'Who is this?'

It was Otis Redding singing 'I've Been Loving You Too Long (To Stop Now)'.

And that was the point at which I picked up and began to unravel that thread hanging just outside my field of vision almost all my life. I became a woman who loved soul music; which in time came to feel like a *rapprochement* with my mum. Something we had in common that I could celebrate and thank her for. Soul music and perfect chips. And two of the first CDs I bought when starting to build up a collection of soul records came from Woolworths in Eastwood.

★

One evening a few weeks ago, I found myself, alone in the house, sitting at my dining room table, crying; sobbing with my head in my hands. The image of myself at fourteen in my mum's sitting room, listening to 'Just Like a Woman' had been in my head and was suddenly overwhelming; like opening up a tomb and breathing in the sad air preserved there.

In that memory I am centre stage in the quiet empty house in a way I never was when anyone else was there.

I found myself wondering what I would have been wearing. I couldn't immediately remember, couldn't get a hold on what I would have changed into after school. But what did come to mind in trying to locate an outfit for that evening was *fourteen…aah…I would have been thin.*

Just as I can't ever remember my dad not drinking, I can't remember my mum not being on a diet. I had been dieting too and lost a stone in weight. I was doing much better on my diet than my mum was. I was much, much more disciplined. Not an alarmingly low weight really but my periods had stopped.

So the body moving about the empty quiet room is thinner than it healthily ought to be. Maybe I am wearing my long skirt, dark blue cotton patterned with tiny white flowers; and my long-sleeved pale blue embroidered t-shirt underneath my white, puff-sleeved cheesecloth smock; everything topped off with several strings of love beads. That would seem right somehow for Roberta Flack opening her mouth to sing me Dylan's beautiful words. It would make it abundantly clear how very far away I am from being any kind of soul girl. I am a hippy chick. I am not my mother's daughter. Lovelace Watkins is tacky and dumb. I am a brainy, thin girl.

Pat can eat one potato more than a pig.

This is what my dad says when he sees her eating. I don't ever want anyone to say that to me.

So I move as far across to the other side of the room from soul music and my mum as I can. And in the process I forget things too, of course, and make my story less complex and less true. I forget how much I loved the Supremes and Diana Ross and Jackson Five records in my mum's collection. Forget that I played 'Baby Love', 'Floy Joy', 'Love Child', 'Touch Me in the Morning' and 'I'm Still Waiting' on the Dansette in my bedroom.

I put Roberta and 'Just Like a Woman' on my iPod and listened really carefully again to the words.

Nobody feels any pain

The house I grew up in was full of anger and sadness and disappointment.

I remember two cardboard boxes at the back of my mum's wardrobe. One held her wedding photos, not a single one of which was displayed anywhere in our house or in my grandparents' house. There she is in her blue dress, one hand holding down her veil in the late July wind, seven months before I was born; walking the planks laid over building work into the church porch. And in the other box was her 'conversion kit' – the little booklets given to her by the priest, one to explain each of the seven sacraments. I asked her once why she never did become a Catholic, given that she must have had to promise to convert in order to marry my dad. 'I never felt good enough,' she said.

I remember the little glass animals arranged across her chest of drawers in the bedroom, glossy and brightly coloured like boiled sweets. She must have been collecting them since she was a little girl. I loved them, loved rearranging them, making up stories about them – a pig, a panda, an ostrich, a stork, a fish. But there was one, a tiny blue and yellow bird that always made me feel sad and incredibly protective.

Nobody has to guess
Baby can't be blessed
Till she sees finally she's just like all the rest
With her problems, her amphetamines and her pearls
…She aches just like a woman
And she breaks just like a little girl

I remember her sitting on the settee one evening almost comatose with misery after a big row with my dad. She couldn't speak or move or even cry any more. She just sat there, staring into space and then she fell asleep.

Oh I must end it
Can't you see it's time for us to quit
If we meet again, introduced as friends
Please don't let on that you knew me when
I was hungry and it was your world

She fed me and she shaped me – at least as much as I have deliberately and consciously shaped myself. I start to see and accept all the ways we are alike. I know she is the source of my chattiness, my enthusiasm, the central importance of pop music in my life. If I had been brought up just by my dad, as I sometimes wished, listening to them shouting at each other, trying to come up with some kind of solution, I would probably still have been a poet but I wouldn't have had such a brilliant record collection.

Talking to My Mother on the Intercom

River Wolton

Her body is completely different from my mother's. She has plump freckled arms, a generous lap. She wears a gold wrist-watch that's warm and smooth on the side next to her skin. She smiles and laughs. She sings. She's always been here.

She gets down onto the floor to play, even though it hurts her knees. She pours out red and blue paint for me to splash onto paper. When my nose runs, she pulls out her hankie,

Let's have a big blow. One. Two. Three.

When it's hair-washing time I lie down on the draining board and tip my head back into the sink. She runs the water hot and cold until it's just right, and scoops it over my scalp, keeping the shampoo bubbles out of my eyes. She rubs my dripping head in a towel and combs out my hair.

Ow! Ow! Ow!

It's a bird's nest! What have you got in there?

She can tell when I'm getting tired. I lift my arms up and she pulls everything over my head. Jumper. Shirt. Vest.

Skin a rabbit! We shout.

She lifts me and Adam into the bath. When I'm ready to

get out I stand up in the water as it gurgles down the plughole. She wraps a big towel around me while my teeth start to chatter.

Rub-a-dub-dub. Three men in a tub.

She's always telling us that we're too skinny, that we need feeding up.

I know that she comes from Kent. She has a mother, a father, a day off. She shouldn't eat too many sweets. Her name is Sally.

I don't realise that she's paid to look after me. To wake in the night if I wake. To dilute my morning juice, to pour milk onto my Weetabix, to remind me to put on a coat.

When we go out to the park she wears a blue uniform. Adam sits in the big white pram. When I get tired I sit beside him and she pushes us up the hills.

You two are so heavy, you must've grown.

At the playground I run to the swings.

Point your feet out, then tuck them back under.

Higher and higher. Into the gasping sky. Slowing down is difficult. The seat wobbles, the chains jangle. I want to get off. The toe of my shoe drags along the ground. It catches. I let go, fall, reach for the earth but I'm still moving. The gravel tears into my skin. My hands are scored with lines of blood that burn and itch. I shake them and blow on them to try and stop the hurt.

Ohdearohdear, what have we done?

She brushes the grit from my hands and knees, washes

them in metallic water from the playground tap. Will the skin grow back? Will she get into trouble?

Children will be children, Mrs Wolton.

She's found the best defence against my mother's perfectionism. She is relentlessly cheerful.

★

In the first year of my life my mother builds a house. In her late thirties, recently qualified as an architect, she finds a four-storey Georgian terrace to renovate and, pregnant with my brother, climbs ladders and directs the sub-contractors. She bats away the anxieties of my father, twenty-five years her senior. She transforms the house into an immaculate showcase of sixties' design: perspex and open-plan. Three bathrooms and two additional loos with sliding doors, slate counters and bright orange tiles. Her office is beside her bedroom so she can work while we're at home. There's a lift for groceries, an industrial vacuum-cleaner system, a dishwasher, an intercom connecting every floor. The staircase to the nursery floor is made from open slats of highly polished cedar. Charging down in our socks, we frequently slip, tumbling into the wall. A nanny or au pair lives in the attic. After Sally, there's Pening from the Philippines, Christina from Austria, Carol from Detroit. The house is my mother's exoskeleton. We hide under the beds when she yells at the cleaning lady for jamming the waste disposal unit or shouts at my friend

Sophie for breaking a lamp. For a big house, there are few hiding places.

*

At the beginning of term Mrs Greenland makes an announcement.

'Now that you're in the top form you may put your sanitary towels into the bin provided in Sick Bay.'

The classroom flutters with whispers and giggles. I'm supposed to know what she's talking about, everyone else seems to. Some things come to light in the playground – pain, mess, an excuse to get out of swimming. The absolute imperative of not letting it leak and leave a stain.

Questions boil inside me. It doesn't occur to me to talk to my mother. I've never seen any evidence that this happens to her. I glean what I can from my friends, while trying to pretend I know more than I do.

'My mum gave me big pads with loops and safety pins.'

'It makes you stink.'

'I know someone who didn't get hers. She had to have an operation.'

'Never tell anyone, especially boys.'

I begin to make sense of the white bags that hang beside toilets, with pictures of ladies in long, ballooning skirts and petticoats. Is that what you have to wear? Won't people notice if you suddenly change from trousers into dresses? Every time I see a female body older than my own: teachers at school, women on the Number 12 bus with shopping bags, teenagers swooping past me at the ice-rink, the same forbidden questions ricochet through my head. They're so loud I'm terrified they'll spill out.

Has she got IT right now? Is IT going to show?

Now and then word whizzes round the Upper Third: 'She's started.'

I inspect Her as discreetly as I can. Is She walking strangely?

Periods. For weeks my only focus. The word itself is obscene, discoloured. I don't understand how adults can live normally as if nothing is happening, as if they aren't carrying this knowledge around inside them. The weight of the secrecy builds until one night, when sleep doesn't come, I sit at the top of the stairs, crying. Mum is two floors down. Plates and glasses clink, conversation wafts upwards along with the smell of onions and mince frying. I'm full of pressure. The Curse is filling my head and chest like a filthy dam about to burst.

She can't hear me. There's only one thing to do. I can't go downstairs because that would mean Dad finding out.

I pick up the intercom and press the buzzer for the first floor. She answers.

I barely get the words out past the sobs.

'What on earth is the matter?'

'I know what happens when...when...a girl becomes a woman.'

The plastic receiver is jammed against my ear, my wet cheek.

She leaves the cooking. I hear her footsteps on the stairs. I'm back in bed, shivering. Her voice sounds like she's smiling.

'There's no need to get upset. Some women make a song-and-dance about pain but it's all a fuss over nothing.'

Months later she hands me a brown paper bag with a packet of Dr Whites inside. I'm about to go on a two-week French exchange. The scrumpled bag travels back and forth in the bottom of my suitcase for several years.

My periods don't start until I'm fifteen. I'm on holiday with my dad and brother, and can't find a way of telling Mum when I next see her. In fact, I never tell her; we have had our first and last discussion about menstruation. There's a growing chasm into which all matters of the body topple and disappear.

★

It's Sunday afternoon. The blue trunk, with her former initials on it, has been hauled up from the cellar to the ground floor. It smells damp inside. There are whitish stains on the leather. From the top of the house I ferry piles of skirts and shirts, ticking them off the school list. Four pairs of socks, fawn. Three pairs of underpants for games lessons, blue. One boater with house ribbon. At

John Lewis I've been measured and fitted in fresh, smooth clothes with creases still intact. Everything is far too big. I've carefully sewn name-tapes into each item, even glued them to the tennis racket and the shoe-cleaning kit. For my twelfth birthday Mum has given me a red leather writing-case and a nail-set with my initials embossed in gold. She's said there is a special way that everything must be packed and has bought sheaves of white tissue-paper for this purpose. She's gone out to lunch with friends. I'm more than ready. The trunk is yawning open. Primed by Enid Blyton and Mallory Towers, I can't wait for the escape.

When the front door slams I know immediately that something's wrong. She totters down the hallway, peers round the door and giggles.

'Oh darling, are you all ready? Haven't you begun?'

'I was waiting for you.'

'We had heaps of champagne. Richard was there. Don't frown, you'll get wrinkles.'

With unsteady thumbs, she smoothes out the skin on my forehead and between my eyes.

'Don't raise your eyebrows either.'

I ignore her. Shove books into the bottom of the trunk. She's delighted with herself, keeling onto an armchair and recalling her days at Roedean: holidays spent with friends because her parents were abroad, tennis trophies, high jinks, war-time evacuation to the Lakes.

I speed up. She hoists herself onto her knees and shows

me how the tissue-paper should be folded to puff out the chests of the shirts, the skirt-waists. I don't want any help from her. Her breath smells odd. Her hands are clumsy. I promise myself that when we get there I'll rush off and leave her in the car.

*

Mrs Turner asks the new Lower Fourths to come to her study at 8.15 pm. Already there's so much to remember – the timetable accounts for every moment of the day. Bells clang up and down the corridors from the early hours of the morning; silences and the end of silences. We cling to each other – Nicola, Emma and I, an illicit threesome in this new world where everyone is paired up into best friends.

We perch on her green velour armchairs in slippery nylon dressing-gowns. The House Mistress has a study, a bedroom and a bathroom to herself. There's a rumour that she's really divorced from the husband who, she tells us, is working abroad in Saudi Arabia. A pair of huge orange-tinted glasses makes her look nocturnal, and she walks with a tilt to the right, her upper body leaning forward. In the coming months I will learn to recognise her silhouette as she prowls after lights-out, an ear to the dormitory doors to catch us talking or out of bed. Compelled by hunger as much as rebellion, I will be perfecting the art of slipping down the backstairs to the kitchen, with its vast humming fridges, locked; tiptoeing beside the shiny industrial ovens to ransack cupboards for their offerings: ice-cream wafers, a jar of Marmite.

'Every night you'll come and say goodnight with the Early Beds at eight, then you're to be in bed by eight-thirty. This year we're trying to improve our house points in the Deportment Cup. May I remind you that hair-bands must be black, navy or brown. Skirts at least two inches below the knee. Tie-pins are compulsory. Jeans are worn only on Wednesdays after supper or on Saturday afternoons. Any problems, see me. I am *in loco parentis*. Now that you've started Latin you'll know what that means.'

It's not a question but we nod. A tear plops onto Emma's quilted lap. We pretend we haven't seen it. Haven't heard her on the hallway phone. Don't know that her mum is coming next weekend even though it's frowned upon for parents to visit before the first exeat of term. I can't understand what she's missing. What does home-sickness feel like? Does it make you want to throw up? Why can't she get over it? There's so much to do here: masses of 'prep', lessons until six on Tuesdays and Thursdays, lessons on Saturday mornings, games on Saturday afternoons, chapel on Sunday mornings. No time to think. Only on Sunday afternoons do the empty hours stretch out while we gorge ourselves on plasticky lumps of fudge until it's time for the Top Forty on Radio One.

Mrs T pats Emma's arm.

'That's enough. Now off and get a nice hot drink in the Surgery.'

★

The army surplus coat stays on at all times. Blazing sunshine or downpours which leave it dank and even heavier than usual. I've no idea how it might get clean, and I never intend to take it off long enough to find out. It soaks up cheap lager, roll-ups, sweat. Is a steel-grey blanket, top to toe. Is as good as a tent when I'm propped up waiting for the night bus.

Under it, a black and white striped mohair jumper that I've nicked from the back of Mum's wardrobe. She never wears it. Too fifties. Just right for me, now that black is in, *any* black – furry, ripped, the older the better. The closest I can get to safety pins is a bunch I've threaded onto hoops to wear as earrings. Black skirt, thick black tights, pointy black suede boots. Black eyeliner coating the red rims of my eyelids. Somewhere underneath are my droopy tits. I'm still wearing vests. There's never been a bra conversation and I'd be mortified to face M&S alone.

The coat's turned-up collar hides most of my face, hair straggles across my forehead, and my neck is swathed in a purple Indian scarf. Om Shanti. Anything to cover the spots. Red, bobbling mountains, they rise on my chin, forehead, nose, back. They can tell when there's a party coming, when there's someone to impress; start as tender pink patches then expand to throb and glow at exactly the wrong time on the wrong day. One emerges on my upper lip and thickens it so much that I can't speak properly. I pretend I've been hit in the mouth by a lacrosse ball. As if you'd catch me voluntarily near anything so sporty. My be-all and end-all is TCP. Surgical Spirit. Clearasil. Warm water. Icy water. Leave them. Burst them. Dab surreptitiously at the blood and clear liquid that oozes out after the pus. Girls' magazines are full of advice on 'Zapping Your Blackheads' but what do you do when half your face swells up on a regular basis? Mum comments only once: 'Look straight ahead, smile and pretend they're not there. That's what I used to do when nylons were expensive and I had ladders in my stockings.'

Talking about spots is out of bounds. It admits they exist. If I stand at the right angle, hunch my shoulders, keep my face propped in my hands, they won't show. Hours in front of bathroom mirrors, squeezing, poking, picking.

I'm passing round canapés. It's an exhibition she's organised at a Bloomsbury gallery. Something to do with Islamic Art. I keep my head down. Olives. Cashew nuts. The hot, prickly feeling of seeing my parents' friends arrive and praying they won't come and talk to me.

'How's school? Haven't you grown! This is my son Tarquin.'

Adam is skulking in a corner. Eating stuff instead of offering it round. Dad is nodding off in a chair.

A woman in a posh outfit pries a square of smoked salmon from the plate. She introduces herself. Diane. Thank God she doesn't know who I am. What are the polite things that grown-ups ask each other? I fake it.

'What do you do?'

'I'm the Fashion Editor at *Harpers & Queen*.'

I suppose I should be impressed but this is all incredibly boring. Is it the best that anyone can do? Get me out of here. I'm going to jump on a bus down to Oxford Street. Hook up with James and Bid. See a band. Maybe score some blow.

Mum enters the room with a tray of drinks. She's yack-yacking away to everyone and laughing. Wearing a hideous green dress. Diane catches sight of her and turns back to me.

'Now *that* woman has style! She's the best-dressed person I've seen all evening. Do you know who she is?'

★

She seems to ride like a Valkyrie, with Wagner pouring out of hidden speakers in the plane trees, while Morris Minors and Mini Metros rear up onto the pavement, drivers clutching the steering wheels, as she swoops through them, her state-of-the-art rainproof panniers full of French bread, Cox's apples and rolled drawings, head high above the traffic, all five foot eleven inches of her Viking broad-boned frame powering into the pedals, brooking no diversions, no pauses, in her wide-brimmed rain-hat and red velvet knickerbockers, my mother heading home on her bicycle.

★

She doesn't take easily to a hospital bed. Wherever possible she sits up, gets out, walks around the ward, goes outside. I bring in as much of her outside world as I can. Gravadlax from Selfridges. Copies of *Building News*. Posters from exhibitions at the V & A. Cases of mineral water. The hospital food is an insult. She leaves as soon as she can after the hysterectomy but has to return for chemotherapy, first one kind, then another.

She remains in charge. Friends beg us to tell them how they can help. She doesn't want anything. She is going to get better. A chosen few may sit with her and read the paper while she reads, or drop off light, home-cooked meals. The notion of alternative treatments is raised. She humours me by agreeing to visit the Bristol Cancer Centre. I go to the relatives' group. She doesn't like the cancer diet. It's the mid-eighties. There's a lot of raw carrots and bran involved.

Peppermint Foot Lotion from The Body Shop. I bring it tentatively, prepared for rejection. Rub it into her long, broad feet, the dry skin around the heel, the knobbly fist of the big toe, bunched and tight where it's been pushed into her beautiful shoes. The arches and Achilles tendons are sore. I make small circles along the edge of the sole and press each toe from its base out to the nail. The air fills with the lotion's heavy scent. My hands are greasy, her feet pink and shiny. I cover each one with a warm towel when I've finished it. Work along the ankle and the shin.

'Ah. Lovely.'

I start on her hands. The nails are tidy and trim with perfect half-moons. She has always had emery boards nearby, scattered on shelves, tucked into pockets. For as long as I can remember, her nightly routine has been the same. Before putting in ear-plugs and covering her eyes with a mask, she smothers her hands with lanolin cream and encases them in white cotton gloves. The palms are broader than mine, the bones thicker. With these hands she has played the piano valiantly while I scraped out a tune on the violin. She has returned my limp forehand with a confident thwack. She has gripped the shank of her designer pencils over the high white sheet of the drawing-board late into the night. She has rubbed my back in small, firm circles as if bringing up a baby's wind, and checked my burning forehead as I sweated out chickenpox. She has chopped mounds of parsley, coming at it from one angle and then another with a long curving knife, until the green heap is reduced to specks. She has stirred strips of pork and celery with soy sauce in the heavy-bottomed orange frying pan; turned the handle of the rotary mixer over and over while I poured a steady stream of oil into the thickening yellow mayonnaise.

These hands are puffy and sick, veins full of the chemicals that have been pumped through her body. Her appetite is diminishing. She eats only the puréed apple that I cook for her. I work between the finger-bones, seek out the wasted muscles, following her breath, pushing gently into pressure points as she exhales.

'How about your neck and shoulders?'

We don't speak. At first I'm too rough. The skull is tender where her hair has grown back. I slow down, stroke and tap. No pushing and prodding here. Her face is soft and child-like, despite the years of powder and foundation. The rituals of cotton wool and expensive moisturisers have served her well. I tuck the fringe back. Her hair is fine, a rich brown. She's over sixty but I've never seen a grey hair nor evidence of dye. I smooth out her forehead, work my fingertips into the lines, down the sides of her nose, around her eyes. The skin is delicate and silky, but even now she seems larger and bolder than me. She casts a wide shadow. She is so solid, so very much here.

I stay out one night at a friend's house. Too stoned to get the Tube home. Arrive back mid-morning, armed with apples, ready to peel, chop and boil them down. She's halfway up the stairs. She has made her own purée. I stammer my apologies.

'We don't need you here,' she spits at me.

*

When Mum dies Sally is the first person I think of calling. I'm twenty-four. I haven't seen her for ten years.

She comes to the memorial service. She's wearing a flowery dress and smiling, standing out from the clusters of relatives, my mother's colleagues, the concert pianist who will play Rachmaninoff on the rickety church piano. My half-siblings ask me who she is; she's terribly familiar but they can't quite place her.

'I can imagine how your mother was. I can just imagine it.'

Dad is delighted to see her. He always finds something to talk about – Kentish news or the hops, his trade for forty years. She goes along with him though he is dropping names that have probably never meant anything to her.

I hug her. Make arrangements to visit. She's running a toddlers' group, her husband and children are busy playing in local teams. One sunny autumn afternoon I drive to her village in my first car. A silver Ford Fiesta with a bent MOT I bought naively through the Sheffield paper. Mum gave me the money before she died. I've been up north a year; I'm halfway through a social work course – a relief after the claustrophobia of Oxford.

Sally and I look at old photos. Her teenage daughter is intrigued that her mum was someone else's nanny. I try and tell Sally how much she meant to me. She shrugs.

'Your parents were still around. I had my days off, evenings off.'

Then a question rises to the surface. A question that has lain dormant for a long time.

'Why did you stop working for them?'

She is matter-of-fact. As cheery as ever.

'I felt I needed a change. I wanted to set up a nursery. We decided it was best not to tell you. You were five; in the first year at Kensington High. I packed my bags in secret. One day, when you were at school, I left.'

She's almost triumphant. It was a coup.

I ransack my memory – there's nothing there. Almost nothing. The dark blue carpet on the attic stairs. The feel of it on my hands and feet as I climb up to look, to check one more time. She fills the ensuing silence.

'Of course we saw each other later on. You visited. Then John and I got married.'

The wedding is vivid. Being the big sister, keeping Adam quiet. The pale blue bridesmaid's dress. The single pearl necklace she gave me. My wan face in the photos, tangled hair in an alice band.

I drive back to London through the Dartford Tunnel. Lose the way. The dark closes in. Headlights flash and fade. I seem to be on the same spiralling slip road for ever.

*

I sit in the high hospital bed with a plastic bowl in my lap. Of course I want her to come through the door. Cathy. I want Cathy. My mother doesn't know. I never find a way of telling her. She dies four years later. So what is she doing, in the half-light of my imagination, in this memory which does not include her, marching into the John Radcliffe in the middle of the night? Only Danny and Nick know that I'm here, and they've gone home. The ward is dark apart from a single point of illumination at the nurse's station. The sister is on the phone.

'We need some sandwiches, there's a lot of failed suicides in tonight and they're hungry.'

My mother strides past her. I could jump out and yank the curtains across so she can't find me. But I'm dazed and groggy, I want to throw up. She comes to a halt; stands beside the bed in the semi-darkness. I can't look at her, but I know she's wearing her brown silk evening dress that drapes and gathers at a low waist. A string of glass beads. A clutch bag under her arm. Perfume, face powder, white wine. She has interrupted dinner to race down the M40 through the west London suburbs, Buckinghamshire and into Oxfordshire at over seventy miles per hour, because her only daughter is in trouble.

'Sorry. That you've had to leave wherever you were. I got myself into a bit of a state. Probably been drinking too much. I didn't mean to do it. I'm going to be fine.'

I don't tell her that I want Cathy here. I want Cathy to know what I've done, to clamber onto the bed and hold me; I want to feel her leather jacket on the inside of my arms, her white shirt under my hands.

Is she shocked to see me like this? I can't tell. I'm too busy making myself as small as possible. Is she wondering what went wrong? Everything seemed to be going well. I had friends. A busy life. Lectures. Essays. Libraries. I'd mentioned theatre groups, women's groups.

Now she's trying to say something. I anticipate it: she will change the subject, tell me about the talk she's been to, that Doris has a new book out but she finds it unreadable, too much like hearing her speak. And Doris does go on. She will say it's a pity they can't paint these walls anything but a dismal pastel green. She will say there's a new *Richard III* on at the National and she'll get tickets for the next time I'm in town.

I can hear her sigh. A forced breath through the nose. The air brushes my arm. I know. I know. I've been a stupid girl.

The words come like an old recording, where the scratches and dust are in the foreground and the microphone has been badly placed. Have the pills affected my hearing? I hunch forward to listen better. Try and piece the syllables together. Her voice is gentler than I expected. It seems that she's been away somewhere and now that she's back there's a great deal of catching up to do. Is she the person I think she is? Can I let her speak?

The words trail off. I want to hold her hand, say, 'Mum, I'm sorry, I don't know what you're saying but can you stay, sit down.'

I open my eyes.

She's not there.

Visit to the Psychotherapist

Anne Caldwell

Mum clutches her handbag and refuses to take off her beige raincoat. This is not a good start. She looks tiny as she perches on one of those chairs favoured by therapists – bent wood frame, a stripy canvas back and cushion reminiscent of a deck chair on the prom. Just as uncomfortable. The therapist is a little younger, a plump woman in her fifties dressed in a modern trouser suit, smart but friendly, with a large necklace of African wooden beads.

Mum's upbringing has not prepared her for anything like this. Christened Martha, she was a scholarship girl who went to Queen Mary's School in Lytham St Annes. There was a photo of her around this age in the top drawer of her dressing table. She has two bright red plaits, a pleated skirt, a blazer slightly too big for her and a big, big smile. She looked like she was ready for anything. Mum graduated from her school with straight As in Biology, Zoology and Botany. I think she would have liked to have been a famous plant collector, or expert in animal behaviour; a female Gerald Durrell or David Attenborough. She should have gone on to university, but this was the middle of the de-mob years. She trained to be a primary school teacher instead. Her mottos in life were: 'if you make your bed you've got to lie on it', and that you should 'just grin and bear it'. So Mum did. Feelings were kept very much under wraps. Or in her case, kept in a stock cupboard full of PVA and sugar paper.

I have been coming to therapy for years, handing over cash each week and struggling to keep up my mortgage payments. I am longing for a cure, but have done so much therapy I know this language is out of date and a cure is not the goal. I must learn to 're-write my script', come to terms with my past, and invent a new blueprint for living. Some days this feels very difficult indeed and I wish I had chosen to become a born-again Christian or Pagan. It might have been easier on the bank balance.

'Now, shall we set a contract for this session?'

The therapist checks her watch. We have exactly fifty minutes even though I pay for an hour. The 'contract' bit has worried my mother. She is beginning to think she might have to sign up for something, like an evening class in how to get on with your angry daughter, or something worse.

'Right. Mrs Greenwood. Don't look so terrified. I will explain. We need to set some boundaries in place for this therapy session, something you can both agree to focus on, reflect on at the end of our time together. Now how does that sound to you?'

Martha looks totally baffled now, and is checking for emergency exits. She has not said a word since we sat down.

'Mum – we just need to work out what we want to say to each other – okay?'

'I don't know what to say, you brought me here.'

'I know. But you must have a view on something. On what we talked about at home.'

'You know what I think. I'm very sorry it all happened. It wasn't easy bringing you three up. I feel like a failure now you've told me that *all that* was going on under my nose.'

Mum clutches her bag tighter to her chest and is looking flushed about the throat. She has travelled into Manchester for my sake, from her small village on the edge of Cheshire *and* was lost for a good twenty minutes on the motorway network. She would prefer it if we could just go for a nice cup of tea somewhere and a bun.

Something inside me springs open like an umbrella.

'Here we go again! The focus is on you and your *failings* and I am meant to look after you. Well I won't do it, do you hear me? I won't!'

I am on my feet now, marching to the window, and I can see the therapist is looking worried. This isn't the way she likes her clients to behave.

A police car wails outside on the busy main street that cuts through Chorlton. I look across at the church opposite. It has been turned into a pub called 'Down Under' and serves kangaroo steaks on Sundays. Next door, there is a physiotherapist doing sports injuries and a Bach Flower remedy specialist. I turn back towards Mum and the therapist. The wood-chip wallpaper above their heads is now looking a bit tired. The settee opposite is covered in an Indian blanket and has a tea stain in the middle.

'Right ladies. Contract, contract. Let's start again. Mrs Greenwood. Or may I call you Martha?'

'Definitely not! I'm Mrs Greenwood...and I don't see why me coming *here* is going to help matters. I don't understand at all.'

'I am sensing some defensiveness here...Mrs Greenwood, is that something you would like to explore?'

'What?'

'I said, should we talk about the resistance you feel about being here with your daughter?'

'I haven't a clue what you are on about. Can't we just get on with it?'

'On with what? Do you want to tell me more about that transaction?'

'Oh for goodness sake! What is the point of raking up the past?'

Right at this moment I'm inclined to agree with her.

I sit down again, on the tea-stained sofa opposite my mum and imagine myself at home in my own space. The tiny red-brick terraced house in Fallowfield I have moved heaven and earth to try and keep now my boyfriend and I have parted company. It has lovely white walls, lots of bookcases and framed prints. I have just got beyond the poster and Blu-Tack stage. I have bought a casserole dish and a decent frying pan. I have six matching wine glasses for when people visit and an out-of-tune piano which I mean to take up playing at some point in the future.

I wish I could just let go of the past. It's like being followed by a stray dog that keeps yapping at my heels. I am scrunched forward on the edge of my seat and notice black biro down my linen trousers. What happened to me as a young girl was anything but civilised or something you can discuss with anyone.

I re-focus on the room and remember what started this all in the first place. That very, very difficult conversation with my mother in her kitchen a few months ago. She had made braising steak. She knows I am a vegetarian. She thinks I need building up, even though I am in my late twenties. If I would only eat her stews like I used to I might get a bit of colour in my cheeks and give up all this nonsense about self development and being a poet and a feminist, I'd meet a nice man, get a good job and settle down.

'So, what the hell are we all going to talk about now? The state of the economy?'

My voice has gone up an octave and my neck is blotchy.

'Hang on, hang on...shall we all just calm down a little bit?' The therapist is also perched forward in her leather chair.

'Anne – let's backtrack a little bit. Can you just explain to me the purpose of you coming here together and what you would like to get out of the session?'

'It was your idea to invite *her* as far as I can remember. I knew it would be like this. I've told you – we're not a family who bloody talk to each other in any real sense. We never have done, and when we've tried, cans of worms multiply until you've got a supermarket full of them to deal with.'

'There is no need to swear,' Mum chips in.

'There's *every* bloody need to swear! If we'd at least had a bit more blue language in the family we might've uncovered what was really going on half the time!'

'Would you like to respond to that, Mrs Greenwood? I can see that you're looking quite agitated as your daughter expresses anger.'

'I tried my best. It was hard. I made sure that we had holidays abroad and that the girls had as much opportunity as when their father was alive. That included the music lessons. If I'd known...Why didn't you...? Oh I don't know.'

The therapist is smiling encouragingly at Mum and I can see that she thinks we're really getting somewhere. I fiddle with my ring, look at the tea stain on the settee, then at my mum's over-stuffed brown handbag with its weathered strap. From inside she could produce anything for a *physical* emergency – nail scissors, plasters, Savlon, tissues, mints, and a fiver if you were short.

I go over to where Mum is sitting, take a deep breath, and stroke her hair. I wish I could tell her it was all a mistake coming here and rewind the clock. Maybe I should never have tried to tell her what happened to me back then. She looks tiny. Like a wren, crumpled up somehow. I know she's done her best. She cooked for me and my sisters every evening after work (even if it was boil-in-the-bag cod in butter sauce and Vesta meals), and managed a roast dinner on a Sunday. She bought us clothes when we wanted them and put up with all our strops and moods and unreasonable demands to be picked up late at night from various boyfriends' houses. It's just there was no room to admit things were going terribly wrong. It would have been like reading out your diary in school assembly. As I listen to the sound of the traffic and the city charging past the sash windows, bits of what I had told her that January afternoon a few months ago drift back.

I remember Mum's kitchen table with its chequerboard Formica top and cruet set. Her leatherette stool warm against my legs. I described to her what this big man had done. The man in whom she'd placed her trust to get me through 'O'-level music. An educated teacher with flannel trousers and pale cream shirts. A musician who could improvise brilliantly on the clarinet and understood the inner pacing of a piece of Bach. How he'd taken a genuine interest, helped me choose my options for school, listened when I told him I didn't want to be a scientist or accountant but didn't really know what to do next.

How the stairs in the centre of his house were very dark and smelt of bulrushes. The candlewick bedspread that was worn in places. Its horrible shade of mustard.

How he liked me to fold up my school uniform on a wickerwork bedroom chair and leave my elasticated belt on with its three-clasped buckle across my stomach.

How I stared at the pattern of cracks on the ceiling and thought of the tributaries in the Amazon delta and a steamboat with twin engines that could take you down to the port near the sea.

How I felt the coarseness of his beard scratch my cheek and the weight of him pushing the springs of his spare bed into the small of my back, his breath smelling of garlic.

How the buckle on my belt left an imprint. Three red circles like a cattle brand on my pale white skin that stayed for days.

My mum just stared into space. Looked across the kitchen table at me as if the sky had fallen in. Just like the children's story she read to infants about Henny Penny. She opened her mouth. Then closed it. Began to load the dishwasher with dirty clothes. Then took them out and put them back in their red plastic basket. Outside, clouds were scudding across the sky and it was beginning to rain. I could hear the river at the end of her garden gushing underneath the road bridge.

I was not sure she believed me and I sat there swinging

my legs from side to side at the table, fiddling with the cut-glass salt and pepper pot.

'Why on earth didn't you say anything to me at the time?' Mum said gingerly.

'I don't know. He said it was all our secret and it *had* to stay that way otherwise I would be in real trouble. I was scared stiff. You were always so busy with your school preparation every night, and taking Mary to Brownies, or Susan to flute lessons, or doing parents' evenings or making food. I don't remember you having a minute to talk, you know, really talk to us about anything.'

'Oh, Anne. I would have tried. Really I would have tried. Why on earth... Under my nose as well! Oh I wish your father had been alive. He would've given him a good hiding...'

She came over and rubbed my shoulder with her thumb and forefinger. A muscle in my leg was pulsing. Outside the rain was much heavier now, bouncing off the concrete drive, filling up the gutters.

★

That journey from music room, up the stairs, to the back bedroom and the ceiling-delta had brought us to this therapy session. Without warning, my mother begins to cry. For the next thirty minutes, I sit near her and watch a reservoir of sadness fill up the room. There is nothing I can say. I look on with astonishment. I've never seen Mum crying before. The therapist hands her a box of tissues from the bottom drawer of her office desk. She motions to me to loosen my mum's coat, and, surprisingly, Mum does not make a fuss. When she's finished the tissues, Mum rummages in her bag for an embroidered hanky and a packet of Murray mints. She can't do up the clasp. The therapist is on home turf now. Brewing tea and handing out tissues is her stock-in-trade. *She* looks comfortable and busy in the face of all this catharsis.

I'm perched on one of the uncomfortable armrests of Mum's chair and she's still weeping. I'm holding her hand and I notice it is marked with liver spots and a pattern of blue veins.

'So much grief, Mrs Geenwood,' soothes the therapist. I could sock her one at this point, but only manage a hard stare in her general direction.

'There's been a lot to cry about hasn't there? Our time's nearly up now. I would strongly advise you to book in for another session, and to come without your daughter.' Her voice has assumed a professional tone.

Mum drops the mints and they scatter across the floor.

'I really miss him, you know. We had such a lovely start. All those concerts and going out for meals. Then I'd such a good time when you were all babies. He was a quiet man with everyone else but could talk to me. All those visits to the cancer hospital. Night after night. When he died I was so angry. I thought: why me? Why has this happened to me? It wasn't fair. There I was with three girls and the house to run and he goes and dies on me.'

It takes me a while to work out Mum is talking about my *father.* She has never spoken so much about my dad in front of me. In fact, usually she never refers to him at all. I feel the umbrella in my stomach close up, and fold itself around a small press-stud.

'Well…it wasn't fair, Mum.'

'No. Not fair. I used to like to cuddle up to him at night, warm myself on his back at the end of the day. You don't get used to sleeping on your own, even after all this time. Even after twenty years…'

'Martha…Mrs Greenwood. Anne. You're both going to have to leave now. I'm sorry, I have another client.'

The therapist is standing over us now. Her beads are swinging from side to side and she's smoothing down her jacket with the palms of her hands.

I feel like a pile of washing you would rather just ram in the drum of the machine and switch to 'quick wash with fabric softener'.

'Come on. We've got to leave…' I get out my chequebook as Mum buttons up her coat and fastens her handbag. My hand is shaking whilst I sign my signature and the only biro I've found is orange fluorescent ink. Bloody typical.

Mum looks like she's not sure where she is at all.

'I'll ring you,' I say to the therapist who is now holding the door open and checking her watch. 'Sorry I lost my temper a bit earlier on.'

Out on the street I link arms with my mother and try to find a decent café I can take her to. It's rush hour now and the roads are at a standstill, the air thick with fumes. I could do with a stiff gin but tea is going to have to do.

'I don't know how you can live in a city like this. Look at all these cars.'

I grip her by the elbow and steer her down Barlow Moor Road towards Safeway's.

'Would you like to go for a cuppa?'

'I don't want any of that herbal nonsense. And find somewhere clean.'

We sit in the supermarket café for the next hour. Neither of us says much. The red plastic seats are uncomfortable and are riveted so that we are an exact distance apart from each other. Mum has ordered a toasted tea cake but when it arrives she spreads it with butter, then doesn't touch it.

I invite my mother back to my house, but can see that she is itching to leave. In the car park she observes the broken glass on the pavement, purses her lips. I watch her climb into her Renault Clio. She has an extra cushion on the driver's seat so that she can see out of the windscreen. My sisters and I used to laugh about this fact when we were younger. I watch her diminutive figure pull out of the end of the road, into the heavy traffic and nearly run after her to ask her to stay a while, give her a hug, thank her for at least coming to try and sort things out with me. I think of the photograph I have of her when she was little, her red plaits and new bike.

I stand in the middle of the car park, near some bin bags smelling of sour food, and watch a group of crows jab their beaks at a Chinese takeaway, picking through its contents with their greedy yellow eyes.

In the following weeks, Mum and I talk on the phone like ice-skaters on a canal that could give way in the middle. We circle round each other; stay clear of deep water. She tells me about my sisters' successes. People from school I barely remember who have married accountants, or become nurses and teachers. Asks me about the weather.

★

Six months later, Mum comes to visit me in Fallowfield and arrives flustered. She's been lost again trying to get here, and tells me a very rude policeman stopped her and warned her about speeding. Evidently she was doing forty miles an hour on the A34 and missed the sign that says slow down to thirty. She's lucky not to have been given a ticket.

'It was a dual carriageway, darling, and I was trying to concentrate and remember when to turn left. He was very young-looking for a policeman.'

I bite my lip and tell her I'm just going to get changed so that we can go and visit the Whitworth Art Gallery. There is a new exhibition of Victorian watercolours on that I think she'll like and that won't offend her tastes. She doesn't want to waste her time on any of that modern stuff. Ten minutes later I come downstairs to the sight of my mum, in her best skirt, on her knees in the kitchen. She has found the dustpan and brush from under the sink. It must have taken some doing because I had pushed it right to the back of the cupboard and hidden it behind a large box of soap powder.

'I'm just giving your floor a quick once-over, it looked like it needed it.'

'Oh for Christ's sake, Mum, get up. I'd already done it before you came.'

'Well you hadn't gone *right* into the corners.' She struggles to her feet and triumphantly shows me the contents of the dustpan which include a clump of cat hairs and some old cheese.

I walk into the tiny lounge for a minute so that I don't completely lose my rag. I have lost count of the number of times my mother has come to visit and I have walked in on her cleaning the windows, floors, moving furniture and dusting underneath or 'just doing a spot of disinfecting your sink'.

I sense Mum standing in the doorway behind me, very close to my back. I can smell her 'Youth Dew' floral perfume. As I turn to face her, she is still holding on to the dustpan and brush.

'Anne…are you still going for "treatment"? I was just wondering if she was helping…helping you sort out…?'

We have never referred to The Visit to the Psychotherapist in the last six months. I stare at her for a minute and my stomach's in knots. Somehow the striped Indian blanket in the therapy room and the candlewick bedspread are all twisted together like tights in a washing machine. I can see my mum's kitchen table and the cut-glass cruet. The salt and pepper are smashed, washing is on the floor and it's damp and steaming and covered in bits of broken glass. When I try and pick them out my hands are cut and bleeding.

'Yes...Mother. I'm still going...I'll be going long after you are bloody dead and gone!'

The dustpan falls on the tiles. Cheese and cat hairs spill out all over the edge of my carpet and down the side of the sofa.

I walk towards her and then stand there, hesitating.

'I'm sorry...I didn't mean to say that. Come on, Mum...Let's just forget it. I'll get your coat...let's go to the gallery, like we said.'

'Well.... Well...' Mum is indignant. She has drawn herself up to her full height. (Four foot eleven.) 'I didn't bring you up to speak to me like that, young lady.'

'I'm sorry...it just came out wrong. It's a touchy subject.'

'I can see that. What an outburst! Well.'

She smoothes her skirt repeatedly, then walks towards the window and looks out onto my backyard. There is a long pause.

'I'll clear up this mess and then I'll go. I can see I am not welcome here.'

'Mum...Mum. I've said I'm sorry. Calm down. Come on. Let's try and have a nice afternoon together. I've not seen you for ages.'

I grab the dustpan off the floor, sweep all the crap up and shove it hard into the pedal bin in my kitchen. I fetch her coat, and help her on with it, first one arm, and then the other into the silk lining. She's stiff in her shoulders these days. I retrieve her handbag, which has slipped off my piano stool and is lying on the floor. I dust it down and hand it to her.

I have no idea where my car keys are, but try and smile brightly.

'Would you like a quick brew before we go, Mum? I've got some nice shortcake in a tin.'

She nods, and sits down on the edge of my sofa.

'I think it's going to rain again, darling...I should have brought a hat. It's always so wet in this city. You've got a lot of books in here haven't you? And all these plants. I bet they take some watering. Ah...thank you for the tea. Did you get the shortbread from Kendal's? I wouldn't mind a trip down there after the art gallery.'

I listen to Mum filling the airspace and think for a moment how lonely she must be, living in a small village away from 'her girls'. I think about her endless cheerfulness and good humour. I think about the fact that she's been a widow now for longer than she was a married woman. I listen to the sound of the rain on the French doors at the back of my house, and notice that all my pelargonia are blooming bright red and pink and purple.

I look down at Mum's feet. Size threes. Impossible to find decent shoes for except in the sales. I will take her to Kendals. We'll go through the perfume galleries to the fourth floor where designer clothes fill the department store with air that smells of leather and cashmere. I will ask one of the shop assistants to ease Mum's shoes off and let her rest her feet on a low-level stool. I will buy her a pair of soft, cream sandals for the summer. Refuse point blank to let her pay. We will find calf-skin uppers that will mould to the shape of her toes, leather soles to let her feet breathe.

The Importance of Tea – and Rabbits

Char March

Easter 1995

I am striding up the hill out of Charlotte Square in Edinburgh – shoving angrily through the freezing Easter air.

I'd been hoping for some relief – from actually having to 'be' with her – by going round the National Trust's Georgian house in the Square. But we've just found out it doesn't open for another two weeks.

I am ranting as madly as any Grassmarket down-and-out. *Not open at Easter! After all this isn't a tourist destination, a capital city, this isn't a place that derives loads of its income from visitors – is it? This is bloody Scotland!*

Behind me, I hear a gasp, a thud. I look round. Fifteen metres back, my mum has just fallen, full length, onto the granite pavement. She is lying face down. Her arms and legs are making feeble swimming motions.

There is that sickening split-second when I just want to run the film back – have her leap back through the air, take a few paces backwards on the pavement, then the film to stop, and re-run, without the trip, the fall, the very obvious damage.

And, of course, it is all completely my fault. If I hadn't

been striding out so fast, if I hadn't just gone off on one about bloody Scotland, if I had been linking arms with her like an only daughter should, if I hadn't just... Mum had tried so hard to keep the others, but she'd ended up with just me.

And then I'm running, my coat blowing round me. Mum is struggling to sit up. I tell her – sharply – to stay still. There is blood all over her face. Her glasses are broken and hang twisted from one ear. Her thin veiny hands are shaking and badly scraped. A lump is already blooming on her left cheek. Her left kneecap has gouged through her American tan support tights, and is bleeding over the hem of her best camel coat.

My fury with her vanishes. My mum – my insufferable, utterly impossible mum who I was about to walk away from for good – needs me.

Yesterday I got off the train from the south at Waverley and she was on the platform – suddenly an old lady. I hadn't seen her for over nine years – since I cut off all contact, sent back all letters 'Return to Sender', changed my job, then my address, then my name. She is much smaller than nine years ago. White-haired now. And thin. And with a smile that looks so much like Grandma's I keep doing a double-take.

I've no idea what she thought of me.

The first hour or so of us being together, everything had gone fine. We'd talked non-stop about seemingly everything. Then there'd been a show that night so we could sit in the dark, next to each other, with no need to talk. Then a night of my mum's chainsaw snoring – and me in the twin bed suddenly wondering what on earth I was doing in this claustrophobic hotel room on 'neutral' ground. Then a dreadful lukewarm breakfast with businessmen settling their porn channel extras at the reception desk beside our table. The attempt at National Trust distraction had seemed the last straw.

I kneel down on the pavement, hold her awkwardly, tell her everything will be okay, to just stay still while I check out her legs. Meanwhile, I am looking through the traffic to try to catch a taxi's eye. I run my hands tentatively down both her alarmingly thin shins.

What on earth am I checking for? Fetlocks? (Whatever they are.) 'They Shoot Horses Don't They' is thundering through my head.

I say: *There must be an uneven paving slab.* And I glare around for the offending edge – something else to blame Scotland for. But the pavement is miraculous – the only billiard-table-smooth section in Europe. There is absolutely nothing she could possibly have tripped on. This makes it, of course, even more my fault.

I'm sure there was something, dear. I think I felt it shift.

She rabbits on while I try to assess the damage. *I must be getting clumsy. Not picking my feet up properly. Getting slovenly.*

I mumble: *I was walking too quickly. I'm sorry.*

Oh, it's not your fault, dear. I should have got my hands out faster. Besides, Jack says I'm always falling these days.

I don't know my mother's 'these days' – she was just into her sixties when I cut off contact. Now she's a frail lady in her seventies.

Of course, not that much about her has changed – she still has no intention of doing what I suggest. She does not 'stay still', she keeps saying *I'm fine, I'm fine. It's just a bit of a scrape. Just a bit of a scrape.* And she tries to struggle to her feet, but can't. This alarms me. On the one hand I want her to do – just for once in her life, just for this bloody once – what I say: to keep still. On the other, I want her to leap up, dust herself down, say *Silly me! I don't know... whatever was I thinking of!* and to stride off to the National Gallery where they do a decent pot of tea.

Two passers-by – very Morningsidey ladies – ask if they can help. They collect Mum's handbag from near the railings. This, I realise, is serious – I've never known my mum let go of her handbag in public. The ladies offer clean lace-edged hankies, fuss and tut in that very Edinburgh West-Endy way – I want to bellow *Bugger off!* at them, but I spot a taxi.

So I let them help me get Mum into the taxi – and all the time Mum's saying *Oh, I'm being such a nuisance. I don't need a taxi. I can manage. I'll be fine.* She is in her seventies and she still doesn't believe she is worth something as extravagant as a five-minute taxi ride. Then, suddenly, gripping the coatsleeve of one of the ladies: *Thank you so much. Gosh maybe I do need to sit down.*

I tell the taxi to take us to A&E at the Royal, but Mum

absolutely vetoes this. She gets so agitated that I relent – tell him to take us back to our hotel. Meanwhile, I take off Mum's smashed glasses, fold them carefully and put them into her handbag. She looks horribly vulnerable without them. Can obviously barely see me. I know how lost I feel the only time I ever take mine off – at the swimming pool. It suddenly becomes a terrifying place of loud slaps on water and shouts and people running past and no way of knowing how to get back to the women's changing rooms.

I hold onto Mum – an arm round her shoulders, and the other gently holding one of her scraped hands – all the way back to the hotel. I don't know what I say. Probably gibberish. Hopefully it's slightly comforting gibberish.

At the hotel I tell the taxi to wait while I get two hotel staff out to help me manoeuvre Mum into the lift. She keeps up her *I'm so sorry about all this. I'm sure I'll be able to manage. Oh dear me, I am causing a fuss. I'm so sorry. I'm putting you all to such a lot of trouble.* If she's not careful, I'll slap her.

Then the doors slide shut and we stand quietly in the lift, my right arm firm round her waist. We watch the numbers slowly increase, and I wonder: *Am I holding her up...or clinging to her?*

Out of the shush of the lift, I get Mum along the corridor, negotiate the swipe-card door and lower her gently onto the edge of the hotel bed. She gives a big sigh, and sits for a moment, quiet, holding her head in her hands while I grab the phone – tell the receptionist I want extra flannels and towels and a bowl of ice. I stare at Mum while I bark out instructions to the receptionist. My heart is eight times its normal size, it is choking me, it isn't allowing any air into my lungs, I have to keep swallowing.

Mum looks up from the bowl of her thin hands. *Could you ask them for some tea? I'd love a cup of tea.*

How on earth could I have forgotten that life-giving elixir – the liquid that calms any crisis? I order a tray of tea and biscuits – *A big pot, and extra hot water.*

They bring the flannels, the towels, the ice, say the tea is on its way – keep suggesting the hospital. But Mum is adamant, so I become her guard-dog – snarling at them, at the very end of my leash, that she's not going anywhere and to leave us alone, and to hurry up with the tea.

Mum's still perched on the end of the bed in her best camel coat. She's soaked one of the flannels, and, instead of mopping at her smashed knee, or her bloody face, she is trying to sponge away the blood spatters from the hem of her coat.

I gently take the flannel from her. Ease her coat off. Give her fresh cold flannels to hold on her scraped hands while I dab-dab at the blood from beside her eye, and hold ice in a flannel against the blue egg lump that is sitting on her left cheekbone.

And we chat – much more easily and gently with each other than we have managed at any time in the previous twenty-four hours together.

I help her out of her tights. This is the first time I've ever helped my mum in any intimate way. Her silky under-slip slides past the backs of my hands. Her tights are warm, with an almost furry feel, at the top of her thighs. It is very hard to pull the thick American-tan fabric wide enough to get it over her swollen knee without hurting her more. Underneath, her legs are very very white and thickly varicose-veined.

Her left knee is a real mess. Cut right through her thin skin to the bone and swelling to well over twice its size. I mention hospital and X-ray and she is suddenly Mum again. *Absolutely not! I'm not going in one of those places. I'd know if it was broken. And it's not. I just need a bit of rest and I'll be right as rain.*

I back off.

I put an icepack on her knee. Then soak the flannels again, and carefully clean up the scrapes in her palms. It's then I remember the little tube of Arnica I've got in my sponge bag. When I come back with it, I realise Mum is shivering.

The room is warm – stuffy almost – but I find her mohair jumper in her drawer, drape it round her shoulders. Tuck her silk scarf round her neck. Sit on the edge of the bed and hold her for a few moments. We don't say anything.

Then I sit on the carpet at her feet and squeeze out some Arnica and start to very gently work it into the unbroken skin of her knee – to try to help with the bruises. I am concentrating – desperate not to press too hard. But then I see tiny splashes appearing on Mum's skirt. I look up – she's crying. I can't remember ever seeing my mum cry before – except at Grandma's funeral, and then, only very very briefly.

I'm sorry, Mum – I'm doing it as gently as I can.

It's not that. It's that you're doing it with such...love.

There is a tentative knock on the door – the tray of tea has finally arrived.

Never has tea tasted so good. We munch through the thick biscuits – Scottish shortbread which we both hate. *It's like eating sugary paving slab,* Mum says.

Well, you're the world expert on paving slabs, I say, and I suggest using the 'complementary sewing kit' (we both tut at the mis-spelling) to create a fashionable multi-teabag head-poultice. *That'll soon have you right, Mum.*

Easter 2008

When I tell Mum that I've been asked to run a writing workshop for families who've had a stillborn child, she goes through to the kitchen to make another pot of tea, leaving me in the back room with the wonderful view of the loch, and this pot of tea, that we haven't even started, still scalding into the thick cork mat.

I tilt back a little in my chair to try to see her. Her back is to me, shoulders square with the sink, the kettle already grumbling to a fresh boil. I even dare rocking back on the chair – French-polished mahogany legs braced in a triple dove-tailed frame, made by her father in the dim workshop at the end of the Doncaster garden that he never got fitted up to the mains. Where he French-polished this table, that I'm bracing myself against, under the glim of three bike lamps, and French-polished the huge sideboard in the front room that is filled with things kept 'for best' and is covered in strange fawn-coloured hand-embroidered doilies.

The doilies were sent from Calcutta by Auntie Elsie decades ago. Their willow leaves are embroidered so fatly that they look like handfuls of slugs, not the waving tracery of leaves. When Mum read Auntie Elsie's note saying she'd bought them to support a leper colony, Mum promptly boiled the lot, and they've never quite ironed flat ever since. There are loads of them – the top of the sideboard is covered in a colony of various sizes of leper doilies: for the carriage clock, for the tall squint stoneware vase I made when I was eight, for the ashtray Mum made at my dad's pottery night class, for the framed photos of Dad in his interview suit and his Navy kit, for every card I send Mum during the year, and, at Christmas, for every Christmas card – as if their thin card could slash the French polish.

Every flat surface in this house is French-polished, is completely incapable of standing the slightest heat, the slightest damp, the tiniest scratch or dent. Every flat surface is a constant challenge and worry to Mum. As is the fact that I don't want any stick of these heirlooms – that I have my place stuffed with IKEA wipe-clean.

So I am rocking back on the two back legs of the mahogany chair – and feeling very very wicked for doing this because *They're a bit of good wood,* and *They need looking after.* And the frame doesn't give a millimetre – or a sixteenth of an inch as my granddad would have known it. And the kettle's long boiled and I can see Mum clearly now through the back room door and her shoulders are still square with the sink, and her apron straps X over her shoulder blades in that over-engineered way of theirs and, as far as I can see, there's no shaking going on. But no washing-up either. And the kettle's long boiled and there's no noise. No sniffing or quiet plop of tears. There never has been.

I didn't know I wasn't supposed to be here until I was twenty-three. I was standing at Grandma's sink, wiping her chipped enamel saucepans dry with one of her worn teatowels, and Grandma just mentioned it – and was mildly surprised when she realised I'd no idea what she was talking about. *Well, I suppose your mum's a bit sensitive about it – because she lost so many.*

I was stunned, but Grandma was completely straightforward – taking it as read that *these things happen.* For my grandma, growing up on a farm, and with eight siblings (that managed to live beyond infancy) these things did. But not to my only-child mum who grew up without even a garden, or a pet.

There'd been my brother – big, and born a week late

(and then only after a whole bottle of Castor Oil to *get your mum going*). And then four years, with at least one miscarriage each year. Mum and Dad had, it seems, *been struck on the idea* of having five children. And we weren't even Catholic.

And then, finally, there was the experimental drug – to help glue me into Mum's womb for the full term. And Mum being told: *Of course, you can't have any more after this – it wouldn't be safe.* And that she had to *Stay calm* and that *Nervous mothers really don't help matters.*

And I had been a rapidly dividing three-month-old bundle of cells inside her when the first Thalidomide baby was born in Britain.

And now I'm forty-seven, and Mum's still never mentioned it. So, I tell her about being asked to run the writing workshops for families of stillborn children, and she sees that I'm waiting for her to say something. That I'm busy doing my twenty-first-century-talking-therapy-I'm-ready-to-listen-to-your-pain thing. And she goes to make that fresh pot of tea. But, when she eventually comes back in (she's forgotten the tea) she says:

It was only two of them that were late on. And the one that came when I was still at home...well, your father dealt with that. He got rid of the mess. He was used to clearing up the mess – because of his rabbits.

Easter 1966

The previous October, we all moved to this cold place: the central industrial belt of Scotland. To make the transition easier, my brother and I were given a pet for the first time – to give us something to look after, to explain the move to.

My brother is nine, I am four. We each have a rabbit. They live on the back lawn, in the separate hutches that my dad built. There is Duke (my brother's rabbit) – aloof, intelligent, handsome, gentlemanly, exactly half of him brown and half of him white as if he'd had a ruler laid straight down his middle. And then Snowy (my rabbit) – pure white in overflowing folds of flab, indolent, bitchy, pink-eyed, foul-mouthed, with huge unruly claws, way too sullen to exercise, and a terrible flirt.

She deigns to listen to the overtures of the wild buck rabbit who comes out of the woods to woo her. Who stands for hours at a time, up on his back legs, his delicate front paws clinging on to the wire diamonds of her hutch. She occasionally presses her bulk up against the wire, but mostly just sits pretending he isn't there – while she paints her nails, and stubs out her cigarette in her cold cream.

We have been putting Duke and Snowy into a long run together every day since we moved here, but Duke only ever shags Snowy once – after fastidious months of understandable repugnance.

As a schoolboy during the war in Sheffield, my dad had bred rabbits – for their meat to sell in his mum's fish and chip shop, and for their fur which he'd crudely sewn into hats and mittens and flogged to fulfil his schoolpals' fantasies of being Davy Crockett. He'd built a triple stack of hutches to line the shop's back yard and looked after them in between homework and rumbling barrels of potatoes for his tiny dad to slice through the chipper. So, when Snowy started to 'show', Dad realised she was carrying a lot of babies.

It is Mum who tells me the following tale. Not Dad. He never mentioned it. And Mum didn't tell me until I was in my mid-teens, and a girl in my class had just been expelled for 'being up the duff' – and (worse) having a bodged abortion.

It is the morning that Dad knows Snowy is due, long before either my brother or I are awake. Dad and Mum slip through into the kitchen. Mum yawns and tightens her thin green dressing gown round her and fills the kettle for a pot of tea. Dad nods at the kettle, says: *I'll do it first.* Mum rubs his shoulder, then reaches under the sink for the yellow bucket she keeps specifically for when Dad is sick with his migraines. She watches as Dad carefully fills the bucket with water at blood heat. Watches as he creeps out over the frost-pricked grass in his slippers, balancing the bucket that gently steams in the Falkirk air.

She doesn't go back to bed, she stands, a pale green figure, watching him through the kitchen's glass door (my dad's vain attempt to bring some light into the kitchen that faces due south but is under the cliff of the council estate ridge). She watches as he cracks open Snowy's bedroom door, and counts. Behind her the kettle boils – and then starts to cool.

He'd known there would be too many – that Snowy, being Snowy, may decide to eat the lot. So he has rubbed an old gardening glove with Snowy's raisin droppings, and now slips his gloved hand into the hay nest, under her yielding bulk, and pulls out six tiny pink hairless shut-eyed babies. And drowns them.

Mum watches him shut Snowy's bedroom door and carefully carry the bucket down the lawn to stand it on the crazy-paving by the bin. He straightens up and taps on the kitchen window. His face is very white. He mouths:

Jolly – can you bring some newspapers.

She takes him out a bundle of *Falkirk Herald*s and a *Scotsman* and goes straight back in – can't watch while he fishes the little bodies from the lukewarm water and wraps them: corner over, roll, edges in, roll, then places the roll slantwise onto another new newspaper, corner over, roll, edges in, roll, another newspaper, corner over, roll, edges in, roll. The movement is a type of ballet – learnt from serving in the fish and chip shop from when he could only just reach the counter – double- and triple-wrapping the steelworkers' fish suppers so they're still steaming when they get them home. Another newspaper, corner over, roll, edges in, roll – until the parcel is as fat as a toddler and he crams it deep down in the dustbin so my brother and I won't spot it.

And then he had wandered around the dark frost-held garden for about half an hour. Mum said she'd gone out to him twice to try to get him to come in. Had even gone up to the far end, with the gentle tinkle of a full cup of tea chattering in its saucer. Up to where Dad stood by his compost heaps. And she'd balanced the cup and saucer carefully on the top of one of the fence-posts and put her arms round him. But he'd not been able to speak, or even drink his tea – just gestured her back inside.

When he had, finally, come back in – weeping – Mum said she'd had to make a fresh pot. She'd patted his shoulders and smoothed her palms across his raw cheeks, and taken him back to bed. And, by the time we got up, Dad had one of his migraines, and Mum was scurrying in and out of their bedroom with cold flannels and fresh-smelling pillows, and we had to do our usual routine of tiptoeing round making no noise – so we had to mute our joy at finding eight new rabbits. *Imagine her having eight babies, Mum! Isn't it amazing!*

Surprisingly, Snowy proved to be a good mother. All remaining eight survived. When they were a few weeks old, and fully furred and frisky, I tried to run a race with all of them. I laid two washing lines across the lawn – start line, and finish line. Of course they went off in eight different directions, which I hadn't ever thought of, and it took us the rest of the day to round them up.

A few weeks later we had found homes for them all. The coalman took the coal black one, and the milkman had the two white ones, and a Dutch art student had the one that looked like Duke (who was, himself, Dutch).

When Mum told me – even though it was all those years later – that Dad had come back into the kitchen weeping, she said it with that clipped, tight tone in her voice. She always sounded like that whenever she mentioned someone – especially my dad – who showed 'too much' emotion. She hated it that he cried. And, as the years passed, he would cry at all sorts of things. He would well up at a film, or a piece of music, or telling us something about his childhood dog, or a sad news story. But Mum never got any easier about it. Always this clipped tone to her voice, this pinched look to her face. This: 'He-absolutely-shouldn't-be-doing-that'.

Easter 1975

I am fourteen. It is still another nine years before I find out about my Mum's miscarriages.

Mum, Dad and I are renovating Edrom Station – turning it into a home. It is a little rural halt in Berwickshire. It's been derelict for sixteen years and nature has moved in. The platform is a carpet of fox-and-cubs, milkweed and sheep's-bit scabious, wrens are nesting in the men's loos, swallows in the old lamp room, hundreds of mice under the floors and in the roofspace. We try our best to work around them – until the mouse pee over every surface, in every bed, dribbled on every plate and mug in every cupboard gets too much, and we set traps that we have to clear four or five times a day, for weeks. Mum isn't unusually squeamish about these – it is something else that gets to her.

It has been a long dry winter, and then sudden heavy spring rain that has lasted for several weeks. Everything is sodden, and all the gutters and downpipes are choked with leaves and autumn debris.

Mum and I are clearing this one downpipe.

There is a smell – clay and animal and wet. A cold smell.

The spring birds are singing:

SEXSEXSEXSEXSEXSEXSEXSEX.

As we clear the downpipe the smell becomes something much more solid – like we are chewing it. It is slimy and horrific and yet, just leaves, oak and beech, some crisp-dry, some fat with rain like layers of rich cake, come out of the downpipe. We reach further and further up with our Marigold gloves and our improvised fencing-wire hook. And then it comes. A perfect nest of leaves and chewed fertiliser sack. The size and shape of a gowpen – a pair of cupped hands. And in it – bodies.

Small, pink, furless, perfectly-formed except for their eyes – over-big and closed but shining black through the pearl-thin eyelids. They are curled round their own tiny hands, and each other. Curled in this nest, constructed with such care in the dry leaves in the shelter of the downpipe just before the rains came. Six of them.

The nest is brimful with water. The smell is atrocious, even before I pour the water away.

The stench is so thick that I only gradually hear my mum through it. She is saying *Oh God* – over and over again. She has shoved herself back, away from the end of the downpipe where we have been grovelling and hauling for half an hour. Shoved herself back on her welly-heels and is yanking her Marigolds off any old way, inside out, tearing at them, and continuing to say *Oh God Oh God Oh God*. Not loud. And not in anything that could be termed disgust. It sounds like recognition. And it's shocking. Because Mum never blasphemes.

Yes, the smell is appalling, physical, cramming itself up our noses, running down the backs of our throats. But I remember thinking at the time: *What's she in such a state about?* I remember looking at the abandoned Marigolds on the soggy grass, hearing her stumble into the house without taking her wellies off, hearing the kitchen taps coming on full blast, and the water running and running and running.

The Gorge

Suzanne Batty

I couldn't stop thinking about the greenness.

Maybe that's when the yearning started, in the midsummer light – all that setting and seeding, all that ripeness and rejoicing! I felt drawn to newness, to a certain gleaming transparency around the usual, household objects. It was my first summer in the new house with Anna, in the heat; there were no fans in the shops, no parasols or watering cans. I had taken to getting up at five, wandering out into the derelict garden in the cool air, the grass high as a ten year old.

I was picking up glass by the old rockery when a man came out of the house next door, which I had thought was empty, and started to practise dance steps behind a trellis where a mile-a-minute clematis was beginning to grow. His bright white, skin-tight bodysuit flashed like a handful of doves against the red wall. But it was the woman I really noticed. I saw straight away her magnificent expectancy. She sat on the low wall watching him, stroking her baby under her taut skin. When they saw me they came over and spoke to me kindly as if I were about to splinter or disappear.

Maybe that was when my daughter stuck her little fingers through the ether and waved.

My mother used to say – don't have children. Look what it did to me. Do something interesting with your life. But I wasn't doing anything interesting. Everywhere I looked, I saw dead ends. Worse than that, I had become a civil servant. I tried to make up poems in McDonalds at lunch time, but there was something about the clocking in clocking out that strangled them at birth. Mostly, I didn't write any more.

On my thirtieth birthday Anna said, 'You might as well give it up. You're not going to get anywhere now.'

She said, 'You're too old.'

I suppose she wanted us to be failed artists together. At least it would have given us something in common.

When I first met Anna, I was almost blinded by the aura of light around her, by her glittering eyes and steel toe-capped boots. But she turned out to be just another of those shiny, annihilating people I used to fall for. In many ways we were a perfectly normal couple. In the evenings and weekends when we were alone together, there was sometimes screaming and once a fire kicked over and once (did I imagine this?) hands around my throat. It was obvious that love had locked us together in some dark, unfathomable way and we had to endure it.

It was impossible to write with Anna around. She sucked all the colour and light and sound out of the air surrounding her. She was like a volcano going backwards and what was left behind was burnt and thin and formless. It wasn't her fault. Her problem was that people had always been cruel to her.

One speechless night, in the brief darkness, I found myself lying in the garden on the warm, cracked path, red brick dust on my face, snails making for my eyes. I listened to all the swollen-headed babies whispering under the hardcore *(feed us, feed us),* their little hands like weeds between the paving stones *(hold us, hold us)* and, out of the chorus, the voice of my daughter saying if you let me come into you I will make you feel placed on earth, precise and sacred, not thrown down, not cast out like a clumsy, jagged thing.

Anna said, 'No.' She said, 'I don't like children.'

Anna said, 'You're just depressed.'

She said, 'Your problem is you've always had people being nice to you,' and went into the kitchen with her cigarettes.

She couldn't help it; a child would have forced her to face the lie she was living. She would have had to face her mother who, after eight years, was still allowed to refer to me as 'that girl'. When her mother came to visit our new house, she went poking around in her shiny, narrow shoes asking Anna what we thought we were doing, two single girls in a family home? Maybe she was right. Two empty wombs with room under the stairs for a pram and room at the table for a high chair and we couldn't even agree on the decorating.

I started knitting little rainbow clothes for next door's baby. I liked the way I could follow a secret code and bring something into being. A bright body, stripy arms, different coloured legs. All I needed was the head and the hands and the heart and the feet.

Anna said, 'It's not yours, you know.'

Anna said, 'We hardly know them.'

She said, 'You're making a fool of yourself.'

When the baby was born I watched the mother secretly from an upstairs window; she walked up and down the garden in the stretched-out evening drinking sharp, clear water and holding a tiny, snuffling thing against her body. I thought about Anna and about my weakness, about my unfathomable capacity for suffering, about my endless reaching out to the blunt saw of Anna's rage.

I knew my daughter had a secret plan, a way to pull me out of sadness with her soft and willing body, with her helpless, needy urgency but I did not, I could not allow her to come. Instead, I went everywhere holding her imaginary hand. At night, I turned away from Anna so that I could hold my daughter against me. I slept in my clothes – I couldn't bear to get undressed. I couldn't look at that stomach, flat and hard as concrete, tiny, citrus breasts, everything sparse and unused.

I bought magazines called *Your Baby* and *Mother and Child* and *Pregnancy and Birth*. I liked the conspiratorial smile of the shop assistants. I looked at the pictures, guiltily; there were women sailing up to heaven like hot air balloons, babies scoured clean wearing turquoise contact lenses smiling, smiling. The lists of instructions and equipment for the newborn appealed to the part of me that fills a rucksack with self-sufficiency and goes off into the wilds. I should have been a solitary pioneer, slinging my daughter on my back, sleeping in a hut on the side of a fell. I could shoot grouse and ford the rivers. We would be warm with unimaginable love on the cold ridges. My daughter would be like herself in form and spirit and no one would take her away.

Eventually Anna said I could have a child. If I must.

She said, 'But I want nothing to do with it.'

I couldn't do it alone. I was afraid. What if she came, not as a baby, but as a three year old with my sister's wild hair, strong and mouthy so that I was afraid of her – that soft, clean mouth really a chasm I would disappear into? What if her hands clutched and clung, her legs astride my back (more leg, more whip!) going around in circles in a small room whilst she threw back bottles of ink and vomited on my notebooks, ate the floorboards and windows, laughing through mouthfuls of splinters?

Maybe I would want my daughter stuffed and upright, dressed in a replica Victorian dress, blinking from the shelf saying do it to me Mummy, shape me and when I looked at her face through my skin it was my mother's. What if I pulled my own heart out through my mouth and there was no blood or milk or words left.

I started to live in my dreams; there was my friend Sonia, waiting to meet me. I was still a child but about to give birth and she came towards me with a red blanket and a shopping trolley *there there* she said *there there.*

I don't know why she said it; after all it was her baby in the tiny white coffin, her city I travelled to, her motorway you could hear from the garden of remembrance. I remember the swollen river, the budding trees, a tightness to the air and the photo of the baby tiny and bruised as if it had been wrung out and flung into a corner.

She tried to put the blanket around me, but I didn't want to be touched, I wanted my body to consist only of the soles of my feet. I walked with her in the back alley and she touched my stomach and said *I'll take good care of her, I was a midwife in a past life* and I agreed with her, I hated the baby, I wanted to hand it over, I wanted it gone.

When I woke up I thought of my mother, hugely pregnant with my sister, keeping to the house and eating crates of oranges, putting her swollen feet up on the table. I remember sitting on the stairs in the night, under my father's copy of *Guernica*, listening to her crying and the grassy breathing of my brother and sisters, wondering what was going to happen to her, what was going to come out and where from? The pregnancy did something to her; she thought in random words – *plasticine, fist, animal, doorway*. Would I recognise myself like that, brainless, wordless as if I'd covered myself in another's flesh, would I recognise the head as it came from the darkness into the blazing red sunlight of my thighs?

I gave up sleeping and wrote all night in the bathroom – the truth, I think, but as soon as the words were written down I forgot them. Every morning there was a vision in the garden – 5.23am every day; sometimes my daughter reaching for my hands, sometimes her body hanging from the washing line. I started to believe that she would come to me accidentally, if I concentrated hard enough – I would see the blue line, I would be like those other women who knew about love, who were miraculous. I wondered if I could fall for a man and practised it in writing.

It was Anna who broke the spell. She went sneaking under my bed, scratching around with her crow's claws, picking through my notebooks and magazines with her scraggy black beak, screeching at me later in the long, narrow kitchen as I was filling jam jars with cut flowers. I didn't like the words she was throwing at me: sick, sad, mental, mad.

All I wanted was some time to look for the truth, some truth, any kind of truth. I wanted to scrape off my skin and find another.

Anna said, 'You've got a week to find some sanity.'

She said, 'You selfish, hard-faced cow.'

I packed the car and I ran.

★

The youth hostel is an old farmhouse with no electricity. There is no one else there, no warden, you have to fend for yourself. Last night I built a fire and fetched a camp bed from the dormitory and lay awake in the firelight with darkness coming out of the walls. I thought of the darkness my daughter would have come from – my own fat, red, muscular darkness, blind and boneless, a lonely cavern in which she would have shaped herself, constantly dividing, constantly put back together, weird little water creature, strong as rubber. Outside it was light and misty, a bird was wheezing in the eaves like a sick child.

Not a soul for five days! My mind recognises only circles the past has fallen through. I come scraping and sliding down the bank to the river following the blue promise of a kingfisher. There is no path here; I walk my boots along under water like a dipper, one foot singing of ecstasy, the other of despair. Look at my hands, one holding death, the other a cord. The trees meet overhead and tunnel me. I will never go back, never.

I can wish my daughter well, now that she's gone back to the wormhole, now that she's gone running down to the foggy beach. We are perfect, she and I, for she has not insinuated her way into flesh, she does not have the cord around her neck or the placenta like a plate of meat before her, stopping up the tunnel of air. She has not been pushed out onto cheap carpet, her nose in the ash and dog hair. She doesn't have to know me, she will not be put aside, handed around, thrown down, smacked on the back of the legs shouted at with false logic, clouted round the back of the head, made fun of, burdened with secrets.

I walk to the edge of the gorge and heave out the great, pulsating emptiness in me; I had not expected it to be so bright, like a glass womb. I swing it backwards and forwards like a birthday child and over it goes down to the trees and bracken and moss to where it all begins. I am willing to step over the edge if that is what it takes but, instead, I think about daybreak, the time when the words come so fast I can hardly write them down, when I am giddy with the light. I walk away backwards. I walk away.

I follow an ancient path to a church on the side of the hill, the rain blowing across like muslin. Out of the weather, a stone font, a floor of rushes and herbs where I sit with this barrenness, I am soaked and battered and still alive. I will not go to the leper's window to stand tiptoed on the slab that holds the dead down; I know that my daughter could never be free of me, my heart full of incomprehensible pain, veins full of poison. I think she will forgive me.

From the churchyard I go, up the slopes of Tal y Fan like a starved horse.

I have a little stone, a smooth grey, egg-shaped stone I hold up to the sky as the wind knocks me over. I listen to the larks and a siren miles away on the coast road. There is a new, clear, singing space in my body; I will not be on the side of endings. I will retreat like a deer into the wood, lay down in the leaves and make little huffs of hot breath in the damp air, little scratches in the earth with a sharpened stick. I will wait for the wind to blow the door open, for something to come in like a bursting of heaven.

Mother

Clare Shaw

I used to hide my head in her lap – the smell of nylon and warm herring – and listen to the foreign language of adult conversation, the coos and clucks and *ooo Margarets.* Sometimes she would stroke my head, her huge hands suddenly gentle. Each day began in the crumpled hollow of her bed, the rain like peas in a can, shaken. Each day ended with prayers sung in a voice as thin as a sharpened E-string. *This is the way of life till the world be done.* Aah-men.

★

I came out to my mother when I was seventeen. One Christmas, some unlucky person bought my father a board game called *Taboo.* This made a fun activity of presenting players with a series of moral dilemmas and evaluating their responses. My father had a violent reaction to the experience of being evaluated, so we took the game home. One of the dilemmas was, 'Your sixteen-year-old daughter tells you that she is a lesbian. How do you react?' I tried it out on my mother who stated that she would inform the daughter that she was simply going through a phase and would get better soon.

By seventeen I'd been cutting myself for years. I'd stay up into the early hours watching Prisoner Cell Block H and slicing my wrists with a thin Bic razor. The same people who told me that fire was hot had told me that being gay was sinful, perverted, unacceptable. Of course I believed it to be true about myself.

But my mother did not reject me. I did not go to school with bruises on my face. I lived at home and stayed up late painting pictures of Kate Bush on my bedroom walls and a mural reading *I am what I am*. I was the youngest of six and the last to move out. My father left and remarried when I was four, after which my mother raised me single-handedly. I preferred it that way. I liked the unobstructed access I had to my mother, when she wasn't working. I loved her visibly, physically. I'd hold my hand inches from my mother's face and beam love at her and she could feel it.

My mother's hands were glazed with hard work and smelt of onions, strong as a hinge. For each of my first fifteen summers, we picked bilberries near Chipping where the moors swang away from us in purple curves and water bubbled rustily from the peat. Where the sky was warm and massive and noisy with bracken and the smell of heather, with the far birds and the sheep calling. I slept with my head on my mother's lap and I wandered and found broken bottles in ruins where families sat round old fireplaces now open to the electric sky, and I always came back to her and she was always there.

Then one day after we'd been shopping I hugged her as we sat in the car outside the house and she said, 'We'd better stop or people might think we're lezzies.'

By eighteen, the phase wasn't going away. My girlfriend, Dawn, was allowed to stay over sometimes in the other bedroom. Mum didn't like her. Not only was she a lesbian, she was also unemployed. Mum and I didn't talk so much any more and we didn't hug. I was offered a place at university and moved in with Dawn. Mum bought me a set of red towels.

The summer I left, things weren't good. Mum was angry with me for holding hands with Dawn in public. Me, I was just angry. We argued constantly about the absolute rightness or wrongness of property, apartheid, the stud in my nose. About the fact that gay people should never have children, because 'just think how they'd be bullied at school'. Mum dropped me off at the university. I looked back at her standing alone by her car. When I visited two weeks later, she'd stripped my bedroom and painted over Kate Bush and the mural. It took six coats of white paint.

★

Five in the morning, my heart echoing loud in the mattress. Hotel room in Ronda, a smell of thorn and rosemary through the windows. Nearby is the gorge where the anarchists were pushed from the bridge and you can still imagine it if you are of the right character which I am, morbid as anything, and it's five in the morning and I should wait. Should go back to sleep but I can't because my blood is multiplying and pushing out from my brains and my heart is a crowded disco with the lights turned out and my stomach is the inside of a lawnmower. My pulse is hammering into the mattress as loud as the café downstairs and the regular rattling roar of the coffee machine which nobody minds because this is Spain, but now it's five in the morning and silent and no one's around except the nuns baking madeleines across the road and the caged birds in the small park crying.

Five past five in the morning and my fingers are discoursing with each other on the nature of reality, on the texture of dust. I am spelling out my name repeatedly with my fingers, recalling car registrations, telephone numbers, making everything add up to integers of five, making everything neat. I should go back to sleep until the hour is more daytime and there's coffee which I can't drink because it reduces fertility which makes me think of trees and sacks of compost and apples and women in canvas hats and not of myself who is most likely made of dead wood and things gone sour. Last night I had four beers – there seemed little point refusing, my breasts already swollen and sore, my stomach rounded with fluid, the red-hot iron of my womb cramping and ready to wring itself out. I could do with a coffee but my heart is as quick as a squirrel's and already it's ten past five.

I touch myself and draw my fingers over the white sheet and look for the stain but there isn't any and my heart is hammering and I'm telling myself to be realistic for God's sake, there's a limit to what sperm can achieve especially when it's left in a pot by the sink in a single hotel room in London at 9am and the morning telly's on and the room smells of sweat and it's the wrong date entirely but you might as well try. I'm telling myself there's a limit to what a body can do when it's been starved and unhappy and anyway I'm Catholic and once I've gone back to sleep and woken up again we can have breakfast and maybe visit a gallery. My girlfriend is soundly asleep beside me and her t-shirt is grey and thin and it's five-fifteen by the light of my phone.

I've done this before, I've crept to a toilet in the total absence of light and pissed on a stick that told me nothing good was ever going to happen. I've waited on stairs, in waiting rooms, I've talked to strangers I have absolutely nothing in common with and for three years I've tried not to hope. Instead there was disappointment so complete it was a deep wood where the sun does not reach, I got lost there. I could not find the way out. It's twenty past five, I touch myself once more and again there is no stain.

The peacocks keep calling and beyond the railings, the mountains where the rocks are cool, and the dew and the pine cones are dropping. Of course there is no life inside me, no cluster of cells like spawn, no spark, no ragged ball tumbling through dark tubes to a universe of deep red light. But still my heart keeps on hammering and my mind will not listen to itself talking sense but continues to insist.

I pull back the sheet and creep to the bathroom over the floorboards, over the cool tiled floor. Helen sleeps on and it's twenty-five past five and I'm doing it to prove there is nothing to believe in, I'm doing it so I can go back to sleep, I'm doing it to put an end to this and anyway I need a piss. Outside a car passes and a lorry sighs, somewhere a shutter rolls open; a room smells of wood, soap, sun. I close the bathroom door and turn the light on, look at myself *hello stranger* and sit down and piss and the stick comes up wet and I leave it and because it will tell me no in one minute, I pick up my book and read. Then I look at the stick and the one line tells me no.

And something inside me sits down heavily, something inside me pulls on sensible clothes and looks at the weather and says ho hum. But now the ghost of a second line is shade by shade appearing and the room is beginning to swing, my hand is on the sink and my heart is a hundred people running fast on a hard road and the line is still getting darker.

I think of texting my sister, how can I be alone for the next twenty seconds while the known world dissolves around me, while the bathroom walls peel back to landscapes I have never walked, where I am a different person entirely and my house falls down and all roads lead to somewhere new? I do not believe in God or in magic but this line is definitely getting darker and my heart is a riot, is crockery dropped, is every radio station speaking at once and by half past five the stick says maybe and I am watching planets spin off here in this small bathroom with the toothpaste and the shower cap. I am the first woman on this new earth, my feet on these first new mountains where the sun is breaking through red orange gold yes.

It says yes it says yes it says yes.

★

You are the size of a large strawberry and around you, I am world. Quite literally. My belly is bedrock and all the night sky. And though you don't know the feel of the breeze yet, I am rain and all of your weathers. What light you have is through my skin. Now you have ears, I am a country in progress around them. In me, strata are formed and exploded. I am river and the way all waters move.

Soon, you will be the size of a lemon. And above you, I will be landscape where factories hum and small towns fume and votes are cast for the wrong kind of people. Small fruit, you are my mineral wealth and you will not be exploited. My heart is an industry that never shuts down. My bad knees are Atlas supporting the planet, and my hands are huge ships that will carry you sleeping, into the night, out into the starlit world.

*

Look what you've got says the midwife. I don't remember her name. I don't think I ever knew her name. From the moment the doctor noticed that I really did need to push, the pain kept rising until there wasn't a thought of riding it, wasn't a thought of any baby because truly I was going to die, truly

all these people and light and me stranded high on a hard, bright bed, and I would get up and leave if only I could walk, and whoever keeps on telling me to *push* does not listen when I say *this is going to kill me*, and look, here is Helen telling me that she loves me and saying

nearly done, nearly done, here's the baby's head, nearly done, and someone puts my hand there and it is soft and hot and completely unlike any head I have ever felt

and I am spelling it out to them as clearly as I can, *this* ***really*** *hurts*, but maybe I have forgotten to speak, I am trying to explain this reasonably, *I am dying* but instead

there is a crowd of faces at the end of my bed looking up at me, staring up at where some natural disaster is surely taking place, where earthquakes are tearing the land apart, where skyscrapers are toppling and lightning is repeatedly striking, where tidal waves are crashing in over and again and I am drowning and these voices are telling me to

push

and not to scream

and here is Helen hanging on to my head and for god's sakes smiling and saying *nearly done, look* and I look down several miles to where the pain is

and there is the baby's head all black and red like an old wound, a new accident, and the baby is wearing me like a too-tight pullover over its head

and the midwife is running her finger round and round inside my skin, stretching it over the baby's head

and there is a crowd of people, the midwife I love and the midwife I hate and all of them still telling me to push, down, and I can't because there is no forward any more and no future, no after and certainly no baby, just the pain and I keep on explaining *I can't do this* but no one believes me

and when I say this hurts they say *good* and when I am sick they say *good* and I am clearly going to die and I hit whatever machine is on my right and I bite the tube they hand me and lash at whoever is holding my arms and I'm not going to push, I'm going to fight, and when they tell me to stop pushing, I push

and now I am burning, something different is happening, now I am the dead centre of the window that smashes, I am a tree where the axehead strikes, now the split second of a head-on crash, the moment the dam gives way

and something bursts out of me, a wave flooding over my thighs too quick and hot to be blood and something solid rips out of me and everyone is speaking and the room is loud and very bright and

there is a baby

there is a baby

and now I remember

and I am saying *oh my god oh my god* over and over

there is a baby

and the midwife is saying

look what you've got, and she says it again, *look, look what you've got* oh my god

a baby

★

For weeks after the event, birth and you laid waste to me. I was all terror and bruises. Like flat land after the storm, there was nothing left standing, no way to take my bearings. I stood in the ruins and wept at the unwashed windows, the meals I couldn't eat. The bed we didn't sleep in any more.

Nothing about me was the same. Some moments I would see my old self walk past and wave, but it was always goodbye. I could not let myself regret a thing, but the grief was a universe I lived in alone.

Now I wear my own body like someone else's clothes. I don't recognise these feet. Somehow, my toenails have grown without me noticing, without me playing any part.

★

It's seventeen years since I left home. Winter is now over. The lambs have moved to the field behind our house, the geese have eight goslings. When I step outside each morning, the air is crowded with birdsong and water. Mum is coming for tea.

I meet her at the bottom of our lane, by the gate that

leads into the wood. She has her good shoes on and is careful to avoid the mud. She's wearing a skirt and a careful layer of make-up, she has one large earring in her left ear. She's brought us a box of After-Eights and three-quarters of a bottle of ginger wine. I'm carrying my baby on my hip.

It's a light spring evening, mild enough for midges. We sit outside where the garden opens down to the canal and watch the barges. My mother and Helen discuss the colour of forsythias, and I bring us ginger wine in tiny cut-glass glasses which Helen and I have to share because we only have two.

Mum has discovered a carrier bag full of newspaper cuttings stretching back over the fifty years my siblings and I have been in existence. It's been hanging around for years, but she says she's never seen it before. And here are the pictures of me, smart in my clever white shirt and neat hair, the mysterious story of my long-distance balloon. My sister's accident, my dead father doing yoga in his underpants. Cross-country results, the time I was raped, my prize-winning essay on the local tip. Weddings and court appearances and births. *To Gerrie and Maureen, a daughter.*

It's seventeen years since I left home. I've had five partners and one nervous breakdown. Things get steadily better, much better. I've got a daughter. I pass her to my mother whilst Helen and I get tea. When I come back, my mother has her face in my daughter's hair. The evening light is yellow and mellowing, a train passes on the other side of the valley. 'She's a very lucky little girl,' she says, and I say, 'Yes. Yes, she is.'

Author Biographies

Suzanne Batty was born in Plymouth, twenty minutes after her twin sister, and upside down. She lives in Manchester where she runs creative writing workshops for people experiencing and recovering from mental distress. She is very committed to the creative act as an act of healing, not just for the individual but in a wider sense. Suzanne also teaches creative writing at Sheffield Hallam University, where she is studying for an M.A. Her poetry collection, *The Barking Thing,* was published by Bloodaxe in 2007. She is the co-editor of poetry magazine *Rain Dog* which was created to get more women poets into print. When she's not writing or teaching, she is usually indulging her dog or neglecting her allotment, or both.

Anne Caldwell was born in London in the baby boom of the sixties and decided to come to the world early. She grew up as a small-town girl in Cheshire and has worked in youth hostels, community arts, libraries, restaurants, and a cake decoration factory. After much travelling and city life, she now lives in a Pennine village with her son. Other passions in life include food, growing herbs and second-hand shops. Her first poetry collection *Slug Language* was published in 2008 by Happenstance. As far as she knows, she is the only writer in Yorkshire to win a chocolate shoe for her work. (http://annecaldwell.net)

Nell Farrell feels her birth weight is slightly less noteworthy than her birthplace, Eastwood, which she shares with D.H. Lawrence. She now lives in Sheffield where she earns her living in social work education and as a creative writing tutor. The rest of her time is divided out (in a not very neat pie chart) between writing, cooking, watching football, reading, chatting, running, lying in the bath with a gin and tonic and imagining she can still speak French as well as when she spent a year in the Auvergne. Her poems have appeared in many poetry journals and her short collection *The Wrong Evangeline* was published by Panshine Press in 2003. She was recently a runner-up in the *Mslexia* Poetry Competition and has been awarded Second Prize in the 2008 *Yorkshire Open Poetry Competition.*

Char March was born (after her mum had a series of miscarriages) with the aid of an experimental drug which unfortunately wrecked Char's immune system, but this has been terribly character-building! She is an award-winning poet, playwright and short fiction writer. She grew up in the 1960s and '70s in Central Scotland. Having Yorkshire parents, this was a wonderfully bracing childhood – given the level of anti-Englishness! She has worked in everything from a brussel-sprout factory to Opera North, and adores sea-canoeing and mashed potato. Char now divides her time between her 82-year-old mum's (in the NW Highlands) and her own home in the Yorkshire Pennines – she clearly has an affinity with rain.

Clare Shaw's proudest claim to fame is that she was the second biggest baby born in Burnley. Described by Carol Ann Duffy as 'probably the best, most electrifying, new young reader on the circuit', Clare grew up in Burnley, spent ten years in Liverpool and now lives in West Yorkshire with her partner, her daughter and various geriatric cats. Her first poetry collection, *Straight Ahead*, was published by Bloodaxe in 2006. She is widely known for her work and publications around women's mental health, and is co-director in a self-harm training partnership (www.harm-ed.co.uk).

River Wolton's birth weight was a mere four and a half pounds but she soon filled out. Born within spitting distance of London's Hyde Park Corner, she grew up in the capital, lived in Sheffield for twenty years and recently moved to north Derbyshire. She's been a social worker, carpenter and therapist, and now teaches creative writing everywhere from primary schools to care homes for the elderly. Years ago she changed her first name, and often answers the question 'Were your parents hippies?' with 'No, I was' (though sadly too young for the Summer of Love). Her latest pamphlet is *The Purpose of Your Visit* (Smith/Doorstop 2008) and she is currently Derbyshire Poet Laureate. (www.riverwolton.co.uk)

Some Girls' Mothers

Futher Information

For further support materials on this book, and for Route's full book programme please visit:

www.route-online.com